Dirty Like Seth

TITLES BY JAINE DIAMOND

CONTEMPORARY ROMANCE

Dirty Like Me (Dirty #1)
Dirty Like Brody (Dirty #2)
2 Dirty Wedding Nights (Dirty #2.5)
Dirty Like Seth (Dirty #3)
Dirty Like Dylan (Dirty #4)
Dirty Like Jude (Dirty #5)
Dirty Like Zane (Dirty #6)
Hot Mess (Players #1)
Filthy Beautiful (Players #2)
Sweet Temptation (Players #3)
Lovely Madness (Players #4)
Flames and Flowers (Players Novella)
Handsome Devil (Vancity Villains #1)
Rebel Heir (Vancity Villains #2)
Wicked Angel (Vancity Villains #3)
Irresistible Rogue (Vancity Villains #4)
Charming Deception (Bayshore Billionaires #1)

EROTIC ROMANCE

DEEP (DEEP #1)
DEEPER (DEEP #2)

Dirty Like Seth

JAINE DIAMOND

Dirty Like Seth
by Jaine Diamond

Copyright © 2018 Jaine Diamond

All rights reserved.

No part of this book may be reproduced, scanned, uploaded or distributed in any manner whatsoever without written permission from the publisher, except in the case of brief quotation embodied in book reviews.

This book is a work of fiction. Names, characters, places and incidents are the product of the author's imagination or are used fictitiously. Any resemblance to actual events, locales, organizations or persons is coincidental.

First Edition May 2018

ISBN 978-1-989273-78-4

Cover and interior design by Jaine Diamond / DreamWarp Publishing Ltd.

Published by DreamWarp Publishing Ltd.
www.jainediamond.com

*For all of you who believed;
there are two sides to every rock 'n' roll story.*

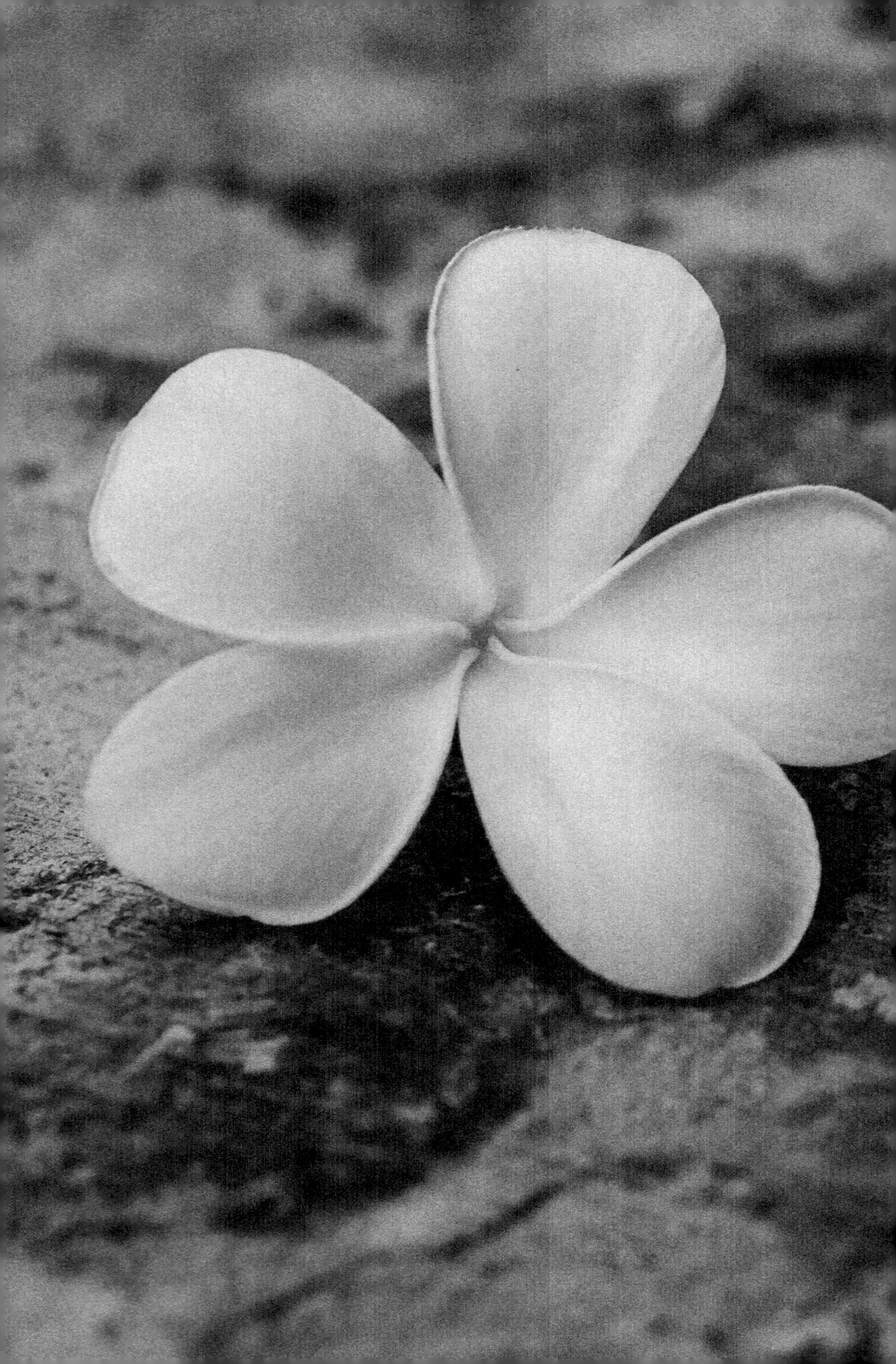

CHAPTER ONE

Seth

I'D DONE some dangerous shit in my life. Stupid-dangerous shit.
Getting hooked on heroin.
Overdosing.
Almost dying at the age of twenty-two.
Yeah; those were definitely top three.
But this, right now, had to rank right up there on the stupid-dangerous list.
For one thing, I was trespassing on private property, on the lot outside a bar owned by a member of my former band, Dirty. The entire band was inside the bar, and while they had no idea I was here, they were about to find out. And I really wasn't sure how they were going to react.
But no doubt, they probably weren't going to roll out the red carpet for me.
For another thing, the bar was crawling with security, and the security guys who shadowed Dirty these days were mostly of the ex-military or biker variety. Which meant a whole lot of dudes who knew how to draw blood.
And last but not least, I was leaning on a motorcycle parked at

the back of the parking lot behind the bar. A Harley. A bike that didn't belong to me but clearly belonged to a serious biker—one of the West Coast Kings, according to the skeletal black King of Spades insignia painted over the gas tank.

It was Jude Grayson's bike. Head of Dirty's security team. At least, I was banking on that being the case.

If it wasn't Jude's, I was banking on, at the very least, that it was the bike of someone he knew, and therefore I was not about to get murdered the instant the biker in question stepped out the back door of the building.

I was doing what I always did when I was nervous: playing guitar. But my mind was on that door. It was painted red, with a security cam on the wall above, pointing straight down. It wasn't pointed at me, but that didn't mean there wasn't some other one that was.

It was early evening and the lot was deserted. There were a few big trucks, the kind that hauled band gear and film equipment and stage shit, and several other vehicles jammed into the narrow parking spaces. But there was a high fence around the lot with a locked gate, and apparently no one in Los Angeles was stupid enough to climb that fence to get in.

No one but me.

I was halfway through Pink Floyd's "Wish You Were Here" when the red door cracked open and some dude's head popped out. He kicked the door wide and stepped outside; he walked right over to me, winding his way through the parked cars as the heavy door swung shut behind him. And yeah, he was a biker. A baby biker. Couldn't be more than nineteen. He had an overstuffed taco in one hand, half-eaten, so I must've interrupted his dinner.

Could've been the dude with the earpiece who'd materialized on the sidewalk shortly after I'd scaled the fence; could've been someone on the security cams. But someone had tipped him off that I was out here. And since it wasn't Jude himself who'd come outside, whoever it was probably didn't recognize me.

Someone new to the team.

This kid, wearing a black leather Kings cut over his T-shirt, a badge stitched to the chest that read *Prospect*, looked more stunned with my idiocy than pissed off. I didn't know him, and whether he recognized me or not seemed beside the point. Either way, his eyes were stabbing out of his head in the direction of my ass, which was resting on the bike seat.

Maybe if I was really lucky he was also stunned by my musical skills, because his eyes kept darting from the bike to my guitar to my face.

"Do you know whose bike that is?" he said, his mouth open and full of taco meat he'd forgotten to finish chewing. Apparently, he was more concerned with my ass trespassing on the bike than with the rest of me in the lot.

I kept playing, looking him steady in the eyes, and said, "I know whose bike it is. You can tell him Todd Becker's here to see him."

The kid shut his mouth, chewed slowly for a bit, and stared at me like he was deciding whether I was dangerous, stupid, or just plain crazy. Apparently landing on the latter, he shook his head. He glanced at the plainclothes security dude on the sidewalk, who was pretending not to eavesdrop. Then he tossed me a biker-brat glare that said *Your funeral* and stalked back inside.

And for the first time today, I actually wondered if this was a giant fucking mistake.

Last thing I wanted to do was get Jude in any kind of shit.

When I first found out about the auditions for Dirty's new rhythm guitarist, I'd planned to head straight up to Vancouver to try out. But then I changed my mind. The auditions were only starting in Vancouver, but ending in L.A. the following week. And the more I thought about it, the more it made sense to wait.

Then I'd called Jude and found out he wasn't even in Vancouver. He was already in L.A.. And that sealed it for me.

I told him I was coming.

He laughed.

Truth was, I didn't think he really believed me.

But here I was.

All week, I'd hung out at the taco dive across the street. Each morning, I watched the lineup of hopefuls grow, winding down the sidewalk behind the velvet rope and around the block. Each afternoon, I watched the crowd dwindle until the last guitarist left the building. Most of the time I'd sat on the sidewalk, playing my acoustic, and even though I wasn't intentionally busking, people had tossed me cash.

That was weird.

I once had a number-one album. Now I had crumpled bills in my guitar case.

The end of each day, I'd bought three tacos and a juice. I'd given them to the old guy who lived out behind the taco place, along with all the leftover cash. Maybe that was just sponsoring an addiction, and maybe after all I'd been through with my own addiction I should've been wary of that. But the dude was seventy-six years old and living in an alley; if he wanted whiskey for breakfast, you asked me, that was his prerogative.

It was several days before I even glimpsed any members of the band.

On Thursday, just as the sun was starting to set, Dylan Cope strode out onto the sidewalk from the gated lot behind the bar—his bar—with a few other guys. The dude was crazy tall, plus his unruly auburn hair was aflame in the evening sun, so there was no mistaking him. He was smiling. Laughing.

Dirty's drummer was definitely the most easygoing of all the band members, and it's not like it had never occurred to me to appeal to his chill nature for forgiveness. Problem was, it would never be that easy. Dylan was a team player almost to a fault; the guy wouldn't change his socks without the approval of the other band members first.

Especially Elle's.

I'd seen her, too, that same evening. Elle Delacroix, Dirty's bassist. Also unmistakable with her long, platinum-blonde hair smoothed back in a high ponytail, her slim, tanned figure poured into a skimpy white dress and tall boots. She'd come outside with a small entourage—her assistant, Joanie, a stiff-looking dude in black who was probably security, and a couple of other women. I didn't even get a look at her face. She'd spoken with the guys, mainly Dylan, and after giving him a hug and a kiss on the cheek, she disappeared behind the building.

Were they dating now? I had no idea.

I wasn't exactly in the loop.

I knew Elle had dated Jesse Mayes, Dirty's lead guitarist, a while back; everyone knew that. So maybe anything was possible. But Dylan remained on the sidewalk with a bunch of guys, talking, some of them smoking, long after the SUV with tinted windows rolled away with Elle.

Today, the very last day of auditions, I'd waited across the street until the end of the day. Until every last one of the hopefuls had been dismissed and wandered away, guitar in hand. I could remember that feeling, vividly. Playing your ass off in hopes of getting noticed, of getting invited back, no idea if that was gonna happen or not.

I'd been in that position several times in my life. None more nerve-racking than when I'd first met Dirty at age nineteen. When their lead singer, Zane Traynor, took me home with him, to his grandma's garage, to meet the band. Once I met them and heard them play, I knew I had to do whatever it took so they'd let me stick around. I'd played with garage bands before. But these guys were something else. And they already had a killer guitarist in Jesse.

So I knew I had to bring something different to the mix.

I spent the next three years of my life hellbent on doing just that.

From that first informal audition, to the last show I ever played as a member of Dirty—the night they fired me from the band—I knew I had to kill it. To work my ass off to earn the chance they'd given me. I had to give them something back that they'd never seen before, never heard... something they couldn't stand to be without.

Just like I had to do now.

And to that end, I'd decided I had to be the very last person they saw today. The last person they *heard*. The very last guitarist to audition for the spot. *My* old spot.

So that no matter what came before, there was no way they could forget my performance in the onslaught of others.

Save the best for last.

That's what I was thinking, what I kept telling myself, as I sat here on the outside, looking in. Just waiting for Jude to come outside and *let* me in.

But I was no stranger to waiting.

I'd waited for seven long years for Dirty to come around, to ask me to rejoin the band. I'd listened to album after album, watched them tour the world, playing my songs, with guitarist after guitarist who wasn't me.

Then that day last year when I saw Zane at the beach... He asked me to come jam with him, just like he did so many years ago. And that jam turned into a meeting with him and Jesse, and that turned into a reunion show in Vancouver, at a dive bar called the Back Door, where we used to play. That was just over six months ago now. Me, up onstage with all four founding members of Dirty—Zane, Jesse, Dylan and Elle—for one song. Our biggest song. "Dirty Like Me."

Then they asked me to come back to the band.

Then Jesse's sister, Jessa, told them some ugly shit about me.

Then they fired me again.

For six months, I waited for a call that never came.

And now here I was. Poised to prove to them all how wrong they were about me, as I played my nerves out with the music. As the red door finally opened... and Jude appeared.

Big, muscular dude. Intimidating, if you didn't know him. Or maybe even if you did. Dark, almost-black hair. Black T-shirt, gnarly tats down his arms, jeans and biker boots.

And one hell of an unimpressed look on his face when he saw me.

He gestured at the plainclothes guy, who was still loitering on the sidewalk, watching me. Just a flick of his chin. *Take a walk,* that gesture said. The dude was gone, around the front of the bar and out of sight by the time Jude stepped out into the parking lot and the door slammed shut behind him.

I'd switched songs, so now I was just trying not to fuck up "The House of the Rising Sun" as Jude stalked over. He stopped two feet from his bike, from me, and looked me over like he was making sure I *hadn't* gone crazy.

"You kiddin' me?" were the first words out of his mouth. They weren't exactly hostile. More like he was mildly stunned, though not as stunned as the kid with the taco.

I stopped playing, flattening my hand over the strings to silence them. "You rode your bike here from Vancouver," I observed. "Took a few days off?"

He crossed his massive arms over his chest. "Like to do that sometimes. Hit the road. Alone. Tune out all the bullshit." He raked his dark gaze over me again. "You bringin' me bullshit?"

"Guess that depends," I said, "how you look at it."

"From where I'm looking, it looks like bullshit."

"No bullshit. This is an audition." I played a few lines from Jimi Hendrix's "Voodoo Child." Showing off, maybe. "I'm here to audition."

Jude still looked unimpressed as shit. "Auditions are closed. Invitation-only. Pre-screened. And I never saw your name on the list... *Todd Becker*."

"So screen me now," I said, still playing, quietly, as we spoke. "What do you wanna hear? 'Fortunate Son'...? 'Roadhouse Blues'...?" I played a little from each song as I spoke. "'Dirty Like Me'...?"

Jude remained silent, arms crossed, dark eyes watching me as I played. The dude was tough to read, but the Jude I knew had always liked listening to me play.

We'd established a game, early in our friendship, where he'd toss a song title at me and I'd play it for him. If I didn't know the song, no matter what it was, I'd learn it, quick. It was because of Jude and this little game of ours, in part, that I'd become as good as I had on guitar. Because if I ever struggled to master a song he'd requested, he never let me hear the end of it—no matter that the guy couldn't strum out a tune to save his life. And he'd made it a favorite pastime to challenge me with the hardest songs. In some cases, songs I never would've learned if it weren't for him egging me on.

"You still into Metallica?" I started playing "Master of Puppets." Not my favorite band, but back in the day, I'd mastered "Master"—no easy task—to entertain him.

He cocked a dark eyebrow at me, so maybe we were getting somewhere. "You remember it."

"Hard to forget. My fingers actually bled learning it."

He grunted a little at that, which was about the closest I was gonna get to a smile right now. I knew that.

"Or how about some Rage?" I switched to "Killing In the Name" by Rage Against the Machine, another of Jude's favorites. At least it was, years ago.

He shook his head, which I took to mean his admiration of my guitar skills was neither here nor there at the moment. So I did what I knew how to do: I kept playing. My talent was the only real card I had to play here.

Maybe it was the only card I'd ever had to play.

"Killing" was another hard song—both heavy and difficult to master. I'd mastered it. I'd played it for him enough times, long ago, that it was in my blood. Any song I'd ever learned was in my blood; once I'd learned it, good or bad, I'd never lost a song. Even when I was fucked out of my tree on whatever junk I was on. Which was probably how I'd lasted as long as I had with Dirty.

Yes, I'd OD'd on the tour bus and almost died. But I could always get onstage at show time and nail any song.

Jude just stood there, that impassive look on his face; a look perfected over many years working security for Dirty and riding with an outlaw motorcycle club. But since he hadn't yet told me to take a hike, I knew what he was probably thinking.

It wasn't so much that he was considering his own ass—how this might play out for him if he let me into that bar. More likely he was considering how badly *my* ass was gonna get kicked.

"You want me to dance for you, too?" I challenged, allowing a little sarcasm into my tone.

Jude remained silent until I ran out of song. Then he said, "So this is how it's gonna be, huh?"

"Looks like it."

"Looks like an idiot playing guitar in a parking lot," he said. But then he uncrossed his arms with a small, inaudible sigh. He was looking me over again, top to bottom, seeming to contemplate how quickly the band was gonna recognize me.

I knew the auditions were blind. But it's not like I was hiding who I was. Other than the assumed name, I was still me.

I'd cut off my hair as soon as I arrived in L.A.; it was fucking hot, but the truth was, I was hungry for a change. A fresh start, maybe. No one had seen me with shortish hair since I was twelve, so that was different. I also had a short beard, but I'd been rocking a beard, on and off, for the past few years, and Dirty had seen me bearded. I had aviators on, but this wasn't exactly a glasses on / glasses off Superman trick. I wasn't masquerading as Clark Kent and planning to whip out my cape later.

This was just me.

Faded Cream T-shirt, worn jeans, snakeskin boots, bandana in my back pocket. Metal bracelet with the word BADASS stamped into it, which Elle had given me when I first joined Dirty and I'd never stopped wearing.

They'd see me a mile away and know who I was.

Seth Brothers.

Former rhythm guitarist and songwriter with Dirty. Fallen star. Pariah. And still, whether Dirty liked it or not, fan favorite. No guitarist who'd come after me was loved as much as I was. No one wanted me back in this band more than the fans. I knew that much from the messages I still received on a daily basis. It was the only reason I kept a Twitter account.

It was a big part of what was keeping me here, in the face of increasingly-bad odds. I was starting to feel how bad those odds were, given Jude's hesitation to even let me in the door.

I wasn't quite sure what to do about it. I'd never expected Jude to be my problem.

"You sure you want this?" he asked me, his dark eyes locked steady on mine. "Now?"

"You once said you'd have my back, when the time came."

"I say a lot of shit," he admitted. "Not all of it smart."

"Then we have that in common."

He grunted again. "Tell you what. You play Metallica for me, you've got your audition."

"Great," I said.

Not great. The only Metallica song I knew well enough to impress anyone—maybe—was "Master of Puppets," and that did not feel like the way to go with a Dirty audition. Dirty was not a metal band.

Clearly, that wasn't Jude's problem. He turned his back on me, a non-verbal dismissal, and headed back toward the bar.

I blew out a breath; kinda felt like I'd been holding it all fucking week.

I stuffed my acoustic into its case and picked it up, along with the other case, the one that held my electric guitar—my favorite Gibson. Then I fell in behind Jude.

It wasn't exactly a red carpet, but it would do.

CHAPTER TWO

Seth

METALLICA?

What the fuck was I gonna do?

As I followed Jude through the red door, I tried to work it out. I'd planned to play "Voodoo Child," a song that not just any fool with a guitar could pull off, because I knew I could kill it. *And* because I knew Zane would be impressed with the ego it took to kill it, Jesse would be impressed with the guitar work, Dylan would be cool with pretty much anything Zane and Jesse were cool with, and Elle fucking worshipped Jimi Hendrix.

So much for that fucking plan.

But I didn't have much time to put together another one. The mood of backstage hit me immediately, familiar and unsettling, as I shadowed Jude. The backside of the building was a network of hallways, offices, and storage rooms that snaked behind the main room of the bar. Between the auditions and the filming of the auditions there were a lot people, security, crew, and others who worked for the band or the bar, all bouncing around in a very tight space, kinda like pinballs. Hurried but unhurried.

I found myself looking for familiar faces. Wondering who I'd run into first—and how pissed they'd be at me.

Though not everyone in the Dirty universe was pissed at me.

Jude wasn't the only one who *might* have my back, when it came down to it. I knew that, and yet, as I looked around... I had to wonder. The truth was, I really had no idea who might be cool with me and who might tear me a new one. In part, this was because, as far as I knew, most people didn't really *know* why I was fired from the band this last time. It wasn't exactly made public.

But mostly it was because I had trouble remembering, even on the best of days, how things had ended the *first* time I was fired, with most of the people I'd once loved like family.

It was embarrassing—fucking shameful, actually—to have to admit that to myself, but right now, I couldn't hide from it.

I'd been clean and sober for almost four-and-a-half years now, since finally getting rehab to stick, but my recovery was definitely ongoing. My feet were on the ground, but my head still wasn't right. Most of my memories from the years when I'd been using were not wholly intact or clear; the ones that had gone and later come back to me were often in disparate, discordant fragments. There were memories that had taken years to come back, and I knew there were some that would never come back at all. And I had to live with that, every day.

It was incredibly off-putting, this feeling... The sketchiness of my own memories, the lack of reliability of my own mind. My confused emotional associations to my old crew, my old family.

I knew I'd disappointed a lot of people with everything that had gone down. Hurt people. People who'd once cared about me.

Even if I couldn't remember it.

But as I passed through the halls, my chest tight, meeting the eyes of anyone who glanced my way, my aviators still on... I didn't recognize a single face.

And somehow that made me even more uncomfortable.

I could face up to my mistakes. I could look people in the eye and take the accusations or the disappointment or the anger, no matter how hard it would be. I was ready for that.

As ready as I could be.

But seeing all these people—strangers to me—working around the band... It just reminded me how much time had passed between us, how much things had changed. Not just for me, but for them.

And for the first time since setting out for this audition, I doubted myself.

Would I really fit in with them again, even if they gave me the chance, like I'd convinced myself I would?

Jude led me directly toward an office, and it was at the threshold, just as I was about to step inside, that I glimpsed the first familiar face in the hallway outside.

Katie.

Jesse's wife.

I'd met her, briefly, at the reunion show in Vancouver. Sweet girl. Big blue-green eyes that were staring at me now. Which meant she recognized me, too.

I paused and slipped my sunglasses onto my head. She snapped her mouth shut, like she'd just realized it was hanging open. She was standing by a table of food with a few other girls I didn't recognize; none of them were looking at me. Just Katie.

I nodded at her.

She crossed her arms and looked unsure. Then she nodded back.

Then she turned away, her dark hair falling over her face, and I followed Jude into the office.

He was arguing with someone as I set my guitar cases down. A woman. Petite and pretty, she had long, sleek dark hair, and I knew who she was.

Maggie Omura, Dirty's assistant manager.

I'd never worked with Maggie. She'd come to work with Dirty after I was fired, but she'd been with the band a long time. Longer than I ever was.

"It's just one more, Maggie," Jude was saying.

"Who?" she said. "What's his name?" She was on an iPad, and hadn't even noticed me yet.

I just stood there next to Jude, and when he said, "Todd Becker," Maggie glanced up, her face blank.

Then she saw me.

And her pretty face frosted over.

"Oh, hell no. How did he get in here?" Her striking, gray-eyed gaze stabbed at Jude. "*You* let him in here?"

"Have I ever asked you for a favor, Maggie May?" Jude replied calmly.

"Oh, don't *Maggie May* me, Jude. You never *Maggie May* me."

"So you can see how important this is," he said.

"Brody will fire me," she hissed. "*And* you." She didn't even look at me as she said it, as if doing so might speed up the firing process. Instead she stared Jude down—not easy to do, since Jude was huge and she was tiny. The two of them reminded me of that Looney Tunes cartoon with the bulldog and the kitten.

"Never gonna happen, darlin'," Jude drawled. "And all I'm asking you to do is look the other way."

"Don't *darlin'* me either," she said. "What you're asking me to do is tell Liv and Brody and the band that we need to keep filming, which is not my call. We've already wrapped for the day."

Liv.

Someone else I knew, from way back. Liv Malone was a crazy-talented director who'd directed Dirty's first video, and I knew she'd worked with the band on a lot of projects over the years. She'd also directed the video for Jesse's solo album version of "Dirty Like Me"—one of the most popular rock videos ever. If she was directing this shoot, that could work in my favor, maybe. Liv and I had always been cool. That was back then, though; I hadn't seen her in years.

"Let me see Liv?" I asked. "Please."

Maggie looked at me, finally. The full force of her sharp gray eyes bore into me. Then she glared at Jude again. "This is on you," she said, but kind of sighed as she turned and strode from the room, like she knew it really wasn't.

"Don't worry," Jude told me. "She's a kitten." Then he grinned halfway, and as he followed her out the door, he added, "Stay the fuck here."

Not a problem. I wasn't going anywhere.

The door was still open, and I could see up a short hallway. A few people passed by, but no one noticed me as I waited, alone.

I looked around the office; it was a typical bar office. Cheap office furniture and a safe. A bunch of tattered band posters wallpapered the walls. I stared at one of them. It was a picture of Elle, the cover of her solo album from a few years back. *ELLE* it said, in big gold letters. Then the title of the album in black underneath: *BOLD*.

She was standing against a white wall, wearing skin-tight white jeans and a white tank top. Her hair was smoothed down over one shoulder and her lips were cherry-red. She was staring out at me, all sass and confidence.

I stared back at her for a moment, the way I always did when I saw her picture.

Then I turned away.

I took my Gibson from its case and strapped it on, and I started to play, practicing a bit. I kept it quiet, not wanting to draw attention.

When I looked up again, Elle was there—in the flesh.

She was standing in the hallway, talking with Ashley Player, lead singer of the Penny Pushers. Clearly, neither of them had seen me.

The Pushers often toured with Dirty, and I could only guess that Ash was here because of Dylan; I knew the two of them were best friends. But it wasn't Dylan he was talking with now, in low, hushed tones—and standing really fucking close to.

I watched as Ash put his hands on Elle's slim waist. As his fingers curled into her. I couldn't read the exact mood of the conversation, but it seemed... intimate.

I looked away, a heartburn feeling rising up in my throat. I swallowed. My hands were starting to sweat and I had to stop playing to rub them off on my jeans.

It was a challenging song. Especially when I hadn't played it in years and my hands were wet.

Jesus, maybe this *was* a mistake.

Visions of my failure, of fucking up this audition and making a total fucking fool of myself, flashed through my head...

But I'd asked Jude to bring me this far, and now Maggie was involved. Liv was about to be.

So fuck it. I was committed now.

I owed Jude that much.

He was right about what he'd said when he fired me—the second time—on the band's behalf. It was never about money, or even about the music. For the band, and for me, it was about far more than that.

It was about loyalty. Bandmates. Family.

And I could not walk away from that without a fight.

I'd sworn to myself I'd never do that again.

But still... I was getting nervous as fuck about seeing the band. About *them* seeing *me*.

I hadn't been face-to-face with any of the members of Dirty since they fired me over six months ago. Since the blowout with Dirty's manager, Brody Mason, at the old church where the band wrote music and rehearsed; when he'd punched me in the face onstage—several times.

I'd spoken with Zane a few times over the phone, briefly, and though he didn't sound happy about it, his stance had been along the lines of: *Not much I can do, brother. This is Brody and Jesse's deal.*

Spoke with Dylan once over text, and he'd said pretty much the same thing.

Neither Jesse or Brody would talk to me.

Elle hadn't returned my calls to her assistant. That hurt the most, actually. Elle; knowing what she must've thought of me after what happened. Brody, attacking me in front of the band. Breaking my nose.

Accusing me of *raping* Jessa Mayes.

That memory made my guts churn now, just like it always did. But that, too, I had to face down. That was part of the deal in coming back here.

Because I could not let an accusation like that lie forever.

I looked over at Elle and Ash in the hallway again... and I could see how she'd changed over the years. Still gorgeous. More so, maybe. More... polished. Glamorous, in her strapless white top, gold suspenders and low, tight jeans, stylishly ripped to shreds. Her long, platinum-blonde hair was straight and smoothed over one shoulder, a single, thick braid weaving the top of it back from her face. But despite the sun-kissed glow to her skin, her glossy lips, her fresh, flawlessly made-up face... she looked weary, underneath it all.

Or maybe it was just the conversation she was weary of.

As Ash spoke quietly to her, close in her pretty face, she just nodded, her mouth tight. And it struck me: that I hadn't been there to see her through all the bullshit that came along with the success, the insanity of the fame.

I'd let her down.

I'd let them all down.

I watched her turn and walk away, my gaze falling to her tight, perfect ass in her fitted jeans. Then she disappeared through a door.

Ash stood there for a moment after Elle left, staring at the wall. Then he turned.

He looked straight at me.

I'd forgotten that I was supposed to be practicing my song, and our eyes met. Recognition crashed over his features and he started toward the open door.

"This what I think it is?" he asked, stepping into the room with me. He looked around into every corner, like he was expecting someone else to be here.

My heart was beating a little too hard, so I took a breath. I had no idea where I stood with Ash. Hopefully not the same place I stood with Brody.

"If you think I'm here to audition, then yes."

He stopped dead. "You're shitting me."

"Nope."

He absorbed that, looking me over from head to foot. I did the same with him. Jet-black surfer-dude hair, piercings, tattoos that seemed to multiply every time I saw him. A serious, pensive look in his blue eyes.

I had no idea what he was thinking. I didn't know Ash all that well, though I'd met him a few times over the years. He'd told me at the reunion show that he looked up to me, musically. Called himself "a fan." Pretty humble that way, because the guy could play guitar, he could write, and he could definitely sing way the hell better than me.

"You here with Dylan?"

"I'm here with the band," he said. "House band. All-star lineup." A smirk crossed his lips. "We've got Raf out there. My man Pepper. We play with the kids auditioning, try to make them sound good. Or bad." The smirk turned devious. "Gotta tell ya, a lot of shit out there." He looked me over again, like he was still processing my presence.

"Today?"

"All fucking week." He crossed his arms over his chest. "You serious? You're here to audition?"

"Yes."

"You pick a song?"

Yeah, I'd picked a song. Wasn't easy to do, since it had to somehow showcase what I could do, impress Dirty, and satisfy Jude's bullshit request for Metallica. But I'd learned, from experience, how to slay even the most ridiculous of Jude's challenges.

"You guys know 'Stone Cold Crazy'?" I answered.

Jude never specified it had to be a song *written* by Metallica.

Ash looked impressed, so at least I was on the right track. "Fucking right," he said, glancing at my guitar, like he was making sure I was ready for this. "You want Queen, or Metallica?"

"I want Ashley Fucking Player," I said.

At that, the smile blazed across Ash's face. He shook his head.

"Alright." Then he took a step toward me, clapped me on the shoulder and said, "Be careful what you ask for."
"You're *shitting* me."
The female voice came from behind Ash. He turned, revealing Jude and Maggie in the doorway... and a small, pixie-like woman with short brown hair and glasses, wearing a grandma sweater with jeans and combat boots.
Ash grinned. "That's what I said."
"Hey, Liv," I greeted her.
Liv just stared at me, but I could see her shrewd mind going a mile a minute behind her little glasses.
"We filming this or what?" Ash looked from Liv to me. He was starting to get pumped up; I could feel his lead singer's ego blooming with the challenge of the song I'd chosen.
"Uh, yeah. We're filming this," Liv said. "Get your asses out there." And then she was on her cell, Ash was barreling down the hall, and Jude was beckoning for me to follow.
Maggie sighed and muttered, "Oh, dear God," then disappeared through a door along the hallway.
Ash went through another door, which had been spray-painted with a single word: STAGE. I was at the threshold, about to follow, when Jude's big hand clamped down on my shoulder and I paused.
"Do me a favor," he said, looking me in the eye. "Don't shit the bed." Then he released me.
I nodded, swallowed, then stepped through the stage door, alone. The door was heavy, sound-proofed, and it slammed shut behind me with a resounding *bang*.
I walked out onto the black stage, the overhead lights in my eyes. The stage was literally black; painted black and equipment-battered. It was a rock bar that had been converted to a dance bar; sometimes bands still played here, sometimes a DJ held court over the crowd. Right now, I was the main attraction.
Though no one could see me.
I heard voices, indistinct beyond the mellow classic rock music playing over the bar's sound system. It was The Guess Who's

"Undun." Which made sense if you knew that Burton Cummings was one of Zane's all-time vocal heroes, and also, that Zane liked to play DJ wherever he could, even in Dylan's bar, apparently.

I could envision Zane out there, with his long blond fauxhawk, lounged back in a chair, arguing with Jesse over virtually every guitarist they'd auditioned. Zane and Jesse could rarely agree on anything; I wondered if that had changed over the years.

With every step I took onto the stage, this shit was getting more real. The members of my former band were in this room. *Right now.*

The heartburn feeling was creeping up in my throat again and I tried to clear it—softly, as if anyone could hear me. At least this wasn't a vocal audition; I probably couldn't handle that.

But no matter how nervous I felt, my hands would know what to do.

As my eyes adjusted to the lights, I saw a drum kit on the other side of the stage, and Pepper, the Penny Pushers' drummer, standing behind it twirling drum sticks. He didn't seem to notice me. He was talking to someone in the shadows behind him, maybe a crew member. Ash was gone, vanished somewhere over there that I couldn't see because of the giant silk screen that blocked me from the rest of the room—including most of the stage and my supporting band.

A couple of crew guys had appeared, scurrying around me, turning shit back on, and someone plugged in my guitar.

And that familiar sound... the sizzle of electricity and the whine of feedback. It took me right back—to the last time I was onstage with Dirty, at the reunion show in Vancouver. And how the crowd had loved it. Loved *me.*

I took a deep breath, letting the memories of that show flood my senses... and the nerves left me.

Certainty settled over me again.

All that bullshit about getting kicked out of the band—*my* band... it was like it never fucking happened.

This is what I am.

This is where I belong.

The fans knew it, even if Dirty didn't.

Maybe Jude knew it, too. Maybe Ash knew it. Maybe Liv knew it, and that's why she was making this happen.

And if that was true, I just needed to prove it to Dirty. Prove to them that I *was* Dirty, as much as any one of them was.

Obviously, I'd fucked up. I knew that. My talent had once made my wildest dreams come true, but I'd let my addiction twist those dreams into a nightmare.

I'd fallen—flat on my face.

I'd failed. Epically.

But my memories of failure weren't going to stop me. Crashing from one failure to the next, hitting bottom, clawing my way back and still rolling the fuck on, stronger than before—that was what it took to be standing *here*.

Right now.

Stronger than ever.

I was a changed man, and I wasn't fucking around anymore.

Dirty needed a new guitarist, but they sure as hell didn't need the Seth Brothers they used to know; even I knew that. Or the Seth who made a half-assed comeback at the reunion show, bent on some kind of closure that never fucking happened.

As I slid my shades back on and got ready to play the hell out of this song, I knew I was ready—more than ready—to take back what was mine. And I knew, with certainty, I was gonna fucking crush this audition.

They thought they knew me...

But they hadn't even *met* Seth Brothers yet.

CHAPTER THREE

Elle

FUCK THIS.
    I was so done with this.
    As I walked back out into the bar, I felt restless and agitated. Bored, actually. What the hell was left to discuss? We were at a stalemate. We'd gained no ground here at all.
    This entire fucking process was a waste of my time.
    Mind-numbing auditions. Listening to wannabe rock stars play song after song. Most bad. Some good.
    A few very, very good.
    Not one of them Dirty.
    We'd seen the process through, for the cameras, for our deal with the network, but off the record we all knew that talent-wise it was down to Johnny O'Reilly or Boz Bailey—a couple of actual rock stars we already knew.
    Johnny, if we could convince him to ditch his other band and join us; doubtful, since they had a song at the top of the indie rock charts this very second and our last conversation had gone along the lines of a three-way argument between Johnny, Jesse and Zane.
    Boz if we could get around his travel issues. As in, he was

banned from ever entering the United States because of some drug charge over a decade ago.

Great news for a touring band.

Fucking awesome options.

If we couldn't seal the deal with Johnny or Boz, it was down to one of these auditions, and none of us were happy with the prospects.

Well, a few of us were, but none of us could agree on *which ones* we were happy with.

I flopped into one of the chairs that had been arranged in a semi-circle on the dance floor, facing the stage, for us—the band and our record producer. We'd agreed, easily enough, that it made sense to film the L.A. auditions at Dylan's bar, because it was the kind of place where we might hold actual auditions, even if we weren't doing them for a documentary TV series. No one wanted to go film in some TV studio or on some fake set, and Zane, in particular, said there was no way he was going to "sit on some fucking throne like on some bullshit reality show and judge people."

So here we were, in old theatre seats that had been reclaimed from some derelict theatre, in the middle of Dylan's place, with a house band onstage made up of friends of ours, and it felt pretty fucking homey—the only weirdness being the film crew and cameras, and of course, the giant screen that had been set up, blocking our view of one side of the stage, where the hopefuls stood to play guitar for us. There were lights behind the screen that tossed a bit of a silhouette onto it, but it was pretty much a blur. Most of the time you couldn't tell if it was a man or a woman or an alien rocking out back there.

Zane had bitched about that, said we needed to see what people looked like as part of the process, but Brody had convinced us to go with the idea, which was all Liv's. And we'd trusted Liv, like we always did.

Blind auditions read well on TV, she'd said. *It'll add to the drama.*

As if we needed anything to add to the drama of live auditions with Zane in the room. And with all of us disagreeing over every single guitarist who played for us. All we could agree on so far were the ones who'd totally tanked the audition.

Currently, the guys were still arguing, which meant even though my head was already on a beach in Kauai, I had to put in the appearance of being *here* until they were done with their debate.

As usual, Jesse and Zane were butting heads. Dylan was sitting back with his mouth shut, and I was trying very hard not to lose my shit. We'd wrapped almost half an hour ago; I'd already wandered off to check my messages and come back. We were now halfway through The Guess Who's greatest hits and they were *still* debating the guy up in Vancouver who'd managed to impress Jesse last week with his take on Ozzy Osbourne's "Crazy Train," and the girl who'd played a weirdly slowed-down and somehow sultry Avenged Sevenfold cover yesterday.

"If she didn't have tits," Jesse was saying, "would you still think she played 'God Damn' worth a damn?" He was sitting in the seat to the left of me, though I'd barely looked at him throughout this entire process—unless the cameras were rolling and I had to make normal.

"She had tits?" Zane said dryly. He was kicked back on Jesse's other side, wearing his trademark black leather vest over a distressed white T-shirt, with low-slung jeans that showed too much manscaped treasure trail. Zane had a hot bod, yes. Did I want to see it? No.

He raked his blond hair back from his face with a ring-laden hand and his ice-blue eyes caught mine. He winked.

I sighed.

I didn't bother mentioning that the girl in question was barely eighteen and probably shouldn't have been here at all, and likely *wouldn't* have been if not for the fact that we were filming these auditions, and "good TV" and all that shit.

"So, if no one slays this thing, where are we at?" Dylan asked, for about the dozenth time this week, weary of the argument. He was sitting to my right, long, jean-clad legs spread out in front of him. I glanced at him and he shot me a pained look, his green eyes pleading with me to help him end this madness. "Do we just pick someone for the TV series," he suggested, "and ditch them after the contract is done?"

"No way we're doing that," Jesse said.

"Why not?" Zane argued. "Who the fuck cares? Ride it out, enjoy the publicity, and fire them if they suck."

"No fucking way," Jesse said. "I'm not sharing the stage with anyone I don't want to share it with."

"No one wants to do that," Brody put in. He was standing back against the wall, arms crossed in his leather moto jacket, and hadn't said much since the last guitarist left. He usually didn't speak up when the cameras were rolling, but now that we'd wrapped and we were still arguing, we were clearly in need of the voice of reason among us. "But we have an obligation to the network. If we can't pick someone, they may expect us to extend filming and keep searching."

He looked to the series producer, who was also sitting back, against the wall, playing with his phone. He didn't talk much at all, other than to enthusiastically kiss our asses at every opportunity, relying heavily on Liv to drive this whole thing creatively.

And where the hell was she right now? She was part of the deal, and frankly, a major reason the network had greenlit the series.

A major reason *we'd* agreed to do the series.

"It's not in the current budget," the producer confirmed, looking at us and nodding eagerly, like what he'd said was somehow helpful. Frank something? I hadn't bothered to remember his name. "But, yes. They'll probably ask."

"Fuck the budget." That was Zane.

"I agree," Jesse said, and I turned to look at him, because agreeing with Zane was something he was usually allergic to. "I'd rather we pay for it ourselves and keep the search going until we find someone right." His dark brown eyes met mine; his gorgeous face was mere feet away from me. My stomach twisted a little, but it wasn't the same way it had twisted when we were a couple. Or before that, when I wanted us to be a couple—badly.

It was a twist of discomfort.

And I wondered: when the fuck was that ever going to go away? Was I *ever* going to be able to look at him and feel... nothing? Nothing but what I felt when I looked at Zane... a completely impersonal appreciation of his male charms—because they were completely irrelevant to me.

I looked away. He and Zane were right, but it was not what I wanted to hear right now. We were all burnt out on this search. Not the search that started with auditions last week. The search that started seven years ago when we lost Seth.

We'd been through eight different rhythm guitarists, officially, since Seth Brothers was dismissed from the band. And none of them had technically *joined* Dirty. They'd been hired on, on temporary contracts, as studio musicians or touring musicians, or they'd played as "special guests" on our albums. The closest we'd come to actually filling the spot was when we'd hired Seth himself back six months ago.

That contract had lasted mere days.

Since then, we'd been looking, fiercely, to fill the void. At this point, we were all starting to feel like we were cursed or something. Every time we thought we'd found our guy, it fell apart.

The documentary series was an idea cooked up by our management team, spearheaded by Brody and Maggie, along with Woo, our record producer, and developed with Liv. It was a good idea, for many reasons. It would—hopefully—create a lot of buzz and excitement when the series came out, excitement that would aid in the launch of our upcoming tenth anniversary album and tour. It also opened up auditions to the public, which meant casting a wider net, and the possibility of catching a rising star.

Hopefuls had been screened by Woo and Brody as the first step in the process, which meant they'd watched dozens of hours of audition videos. The best, and in some cases, the worst—this was TV, after all—were invited to audition for the band. Today was the last day of auditions and, to date, we had *maybe* a half-dozen half-decent prospects, but no real contenders.

We'd all entered this thing a little guarded, since it was for TV. But we were hopeful, too. Excited and optimistic about the talent we might discover. And there had been many talented guitarists who'd played for us. Some incredible stories from people who'd traveled halfway around the world to be here.

But no one who'd rocked all our socks off.

Everyone in the band was stressed out by now, frustrated over the failure to find a replacement for Seth, and it was coming out in tension between us.

The guys had continued bickering, but I'd managed to kinda tune them out. "American Woman" had just kicked in, and I'd started to zone right out to it when the music stopped and a voice said, "We've got one more." It was Liv, over the sound system, like the voice of God.

Zane picked up his mic; it was still on. "Is she hot?" he asked into the ether.

Brody walked over, took Zane's mic from him and spoke into it. "We're done here."

"Trust me," Liv said, with her dry-as-hell tone. "You wanna hear this one."

Zane's blue eyes met mine and his pierced eyebrow went up; I could see the spark of interest in them. He mouthed, *What the fuck?* at me, but I just shrugged.

Next to me, Jesse dropped his head back on his chair, his dark curls spilling over the back; his hair was getting long. It looked good on him.

I looked away. We'd been broken up for well over a year, and it was still hard, most of the time, to look at him for more than a few seconds.

On my other side, I could feel Dylan's inaudible sigh. His boots tapped a restless rhythm on the floor, his knees bouncing up and down, and it wasn't just because the man had drums constantly playing in his head. I knew he was dying to get the fuck out of here, but he didn't say anything.

Zane took the mic back from Brody and told him, "Sit your ass down, boss. I wanna hear this hot chick play."

I rolled my eyes. We'd had every age, gender and body type play for us, but in Zane's mind, they were all hot chicks. Until the screen swept aside and revealed that they weren't.

Liv's crew had discreetly materialized from the shadows and was firing up their equipment. I could see her Director of Photography, ready for action, and operators at all the cameras. Liv herself had reappeared and took her place at the row of monitors next to the DOP.

This had to be good, I supposed, or she wouldn't have sent her guys back to work when they'd already headed out to eat before tearing down.

Brody faded back to his post by the wall, and Dylan managed to drag himself to a more-or-less upright position.

All the stage lights that had been dimmed lit up, and the house band got into place. Ash was at his mic, sleek and sexy in his tight black jeans and Ramones T-shirt, his black hair artfully mussed and his piercings sparking in the light. He had new ink on his arm; a white-blonde mermaid that he swore up and down had nothing to do with me.

When he looked at me, he licked his lip deliberately, his eyes holding on me too long, and I bristled a little. He was getting a little too familiar lately, and flirty, in front of my band. And now there were cameras on him, too.

No way Liv was gonna miss that lick.

The lights beyond the screen went up, and there was the mysterious blur that was our next, and last, audition.

At least I fucking hoped it was the last.

Liv cued the band as soon as we were rolling, and they kicked into a song. It was "Stone Cold Crazy." And it was *loud*. Fast and tight, especially given the fact that the band probably hadn't rehearsed it together lately—or at all.

But these guys were pros.

Impressively, our mystery guitarist held his, or her, own.

Within seconds, Zane was on his feet. Even Jesse twitched a little in his seat, leaning forward. He closed his eyes and listened.

The guitarist was good. *Really* good. Somehow, he or she was trading off solo riffs with Raf, without even being able to see him. You could just *feel* everyone—us, the band onstage, even the crew and security guys who were standing around watching from the shadows—getting sucked up into the vibe.

Toward the end, Zane leapt up onstage and started singing with Ash. The two of them totally slayed the end of the song, and when it finished, Zane crushed Ash in a big man hug, laughing. "Hells yeah," he growled into the mic. "Nailed it."

"Booooo," Jesse taunted.

"Sit your ass down!" I called out. I knew from where he was standing Zane couldn't see behind the screen, but it was probably killing him not to go barreling back there and see who it was.

He hopped down from the stage, swaggered on over, high-fived Dylan, and dropped back into his seat.

"So at least we're sure Zane's in the band," I said dryly.

"Like what you heard, Elle?" Zane asked, panting from the exertion of his performance. He was gleaming with sweat as he swiped his blond hair out of his eye; Zane went straight to eleven anytime he took a stage.

And, yeah. Obviously I liked it. We all did.

We all just kinda stared at each other. Zane grinned, but no one said a thing. Pretty sure at this point we were communicating telepathically. It happened, now and then, after playing and creating and touring together for so long.

Synchronicity.

We'd *all* liked this one. Even Jesse didn't have a critical word to say. Yet.

Shit... Had we just found our guy at the eleventh hour?

"Remind you of anyone?" Woo put in. Our record producer, on the other side of Zane, had been sitting back, pretty quiet most of the time, laughing more than talking. His name was David Worster, but everyone since the beginning of time had called him Woo. He'd been like a fifth member of our band in the recording studio, even playing some guitar on certain songs when we needed it over the years. He'd been with us since the beginning, and we'd recorded three of our four albums with him—our best albums. So his voice, when he used it, carried weight.

"Shit, yeah," Zane said, breaking the loaded silence. "Reminds me of Seth."

No one else seemed to want to say it.

"So, now may be a good time to ask yourselves," Woo said. "Do you want a Seth Brothers fanboy?"

"Could be a fan*woman*," I said. Why did they always just assume the best guitarists were guys?

"Could be," Woo agreed.

"It's a dude," Zane said. "He's got broad shoulders."

"You can't see shit through that screen," Jesse pointed out.

"And maybe *she* has broad shoulders," I said.

"And who the fuck cares if he's a fanboy?" Zane added. "He's hired."

"He's as good as Seth," I agreed, "why wouldn't we want him? Or her?"

"Unless he's fugly or something," Zane amended, "he's hired."

"Whoever he is, he's good," Jesse said mildly. He'd been mild about this whole process, reserving his enthusiasm. Maybe because he was our lead guitarist, Jesse had been the hardest one to win over.

But this guy—or girl—*was* good.

Better than good.

Dylan still had his jaw on the floor, so I gave him a jab. "Pick it up, baby, you're drawing flies."

"Say something!" Zane produced a drumstick out of nowhere and threw it at him.

Dylan caught the drumstick without even looking. He shut his mouth, slowly. Then he said, "Think I'm having a 'Devil Went Down to Georgia' moment."

Zane whooped with laughter, elated.

"You have any questions for our mystery guitarist?" Liv

prompted us. She was holding a mic of her own. She hadn't appeared on-camera, but she spoke to us sometimes, prompting our conversations. "You know he can hear you right now."

"Yeah," Zane growled into his mic, addressing the guitarist. "Dylan wants to know if you sold your soul to the devil, or what?"

"Not that I recall," a male voice said.

And we all went still.

Because we all knew that voice.

I knew, when I looked around at my band, that we all recognized it. We all heard *him*.

Liv gave the cue for the screen to move, and as it slid aside, we all saw him, too.

Seth Brothers.

My heart skipped a beat.

CHAPTER FOUR

Elle

SETH STOOD ONSTAGE with a white Gibson Les Paul slung over his shoulders, one hand resting on the guitar neck, the other one twiddling with his pick.

He looked... different.

He had a short beard, but I'd seen him with a beard earlier this year. It was his hair; it took me a moment to realize it. His trademark wavy, sun-bleached brown hair had been chopped off, and what was left behind was darker. I'd never seen Seth with short hair. It made his handsome features more prominent, especially his cheekbones and full lips. He was wearing mirrored aviator sunglasses, and I could not read the expression on his face, but his shoulders looked loose; you couldn't play guitar like that if you were a ball of nerves.

I watched as he took off his sunglasses and slipped them onto the neckline of his T-shirt. Then he looked out at us, waiting.

And it struck me when I saw the look in his eyes: he still *wanted* us.

And I could not get over the shock of it.

He still wanted to play with us. He still wanted to be in the band.

He'd just come to audition for us, and for some reason, someone had let him in and *let* him audition.

And all I could think as I stared at him was: *Why?*

But even through the shock of it, I felt... relieved?

Confused, yes.

And angry.

I felt a whole torrent of unpleasant emotions broiling to the surface.

I looked around at the guys; Brody and Jesse were *definitely* angry.

Leave it to Zane, though, to look fucking thrilled.

Dylan just looked uncomfortable, like he had throughout the entire Seth ordeal.

It was the look on Jesse's face, though, that bothered me the most. "Jesse?" I asked quietly. I did not say it into my mic; I had the thing gripped in my lap.

Jesse just stared at Seth and said, "Get him out of here." He didn't raise his mic, either. But it was all Brody needed to hear.

I didn't even want to look at Brody's face. One glance was enough.

I heard him coming, storming over. "Where the fuck is Jude?" Jude was standing back against the far wall, arms crossed over his chest, where he'd been listening to everything. When Brody saw him there, he growled, "Get him off the fucking property."

Jude nodded his dark head at Brody, then looked at the rest of us. At Jesse. When none of us spoke, Jude's shoulders dropped a bit. He uncrossed his arms and headed up the stairs to the stage. Seth didn't even look at him. He was still looking at us.

His eyes locked with mine, and my stomach clenched.

He was a good distance from me, but something changed in his eyes as he looked at me. As he scanned the expression on my face, processing it. I saw it; I felt it, as he looked back at me. Something there, some kind of spark, the adrenalin of rocking out that song... a gleam of something, maybe—hope?—snuffed out.

"It's okay," he said, clearing his throat a little and finally looking at Jude. "I'll go."

Then I had to look away. I couldn't watch. I did not want to see Jude manhandling him out of here, though I doubted Seth would put up any kind of physical fight if he did. It just wasn't his style.

I felt *sick*.

I heard them leave, Seth and Jude, through a rear door off the stage. The door shut, loud in the silence of the cavernous room.

"The prodigal son returns…"

It was Woo who broke the jagged silence. No one else seemed able to speak.

But Woo was the only one sitting here who didn't know why Seth was kicked out of the band this year—what happened between Seth and Jesse's sister, Jessa, years ago. What Brody said had happened.

"Whoever you choose," Woo went on, quietly, when no one spoke up, "they've got to be on level with the four of you. They've got to be a rock star if they're gonna hold permanent residence in this band. They've gotta have that thing you've all got. That thing you just saw up onstage. That thing you *felt* when Seth played. Seth Brothers has that thing." He paused, looking at each of us, then sighed in resignation when we still didn't speak. "Just too bad his star burned out so soon," he finished.

And that was when Brody said, "We need to stop filming."

So they stopped.

Jude had reappeared, and on Brody's orders, he and his guys cleared absolutely everyone out of the bar—leaving no one but Dirty, Brody and Maggie.

When we were alone, I said, "You know everyone's going to think we set that up."

"Doesn't matter," Jesse said. "It's not going in the show anyway. Seth's not part of this."

"No," Brody said. "But we should keep it. It's gotta be addressed somehow, and now Woo has done that for us, so the rest of you don't have to. Seth had his audition; he didn't make the cut. This is closure for the fans. He's never coming back. "

"Or we could just give him a chance," Zane said.

Brody's reaction was almost painful to watch. He stiffened, his jaw turned to granite, and I didn't think I'd ever seen him look at Zane like that—like he wanted to bitch slap the words right out of his mouth.

"Does anyone actually *want* Seth here?" Brody ground out, in a tight, scary-low voice. I'd only heard him take that tone once before, many years ago; when he'd informed us that Jessa wasn't coming on the first world tour, that she was leaving the band. Unforgettable, since it sent shivers down my spine, just like it did now.

"No. Fucking. Way." Jesse was first to speak up.

"So it's just up to you?" Zane said.

"No." Jesse didn't sound quite as livid as Brody, but he was definitely reigning back his agitation. "We've always operated democratically. If you want to formally vote him out, we will."

"No," I corrected Jesse, "we've always operated unanimously."

"She's right." Dylan backed me up, which he often did when the other two were getting out of hand. "We're all in or it's not happening."

"Who the hell is in, other than Zane?" Jesse looked around at us with dark, accusing eyes. I wanted to sink into my seat and disappear, but I stayed right where I was. It always made me uncomfortable when Jesse was mad at me, but I'd just have to deal with it; I was uncomfortable around him anyway.

"I didn't say I'm *in*," Zane said cooly. "I just said *maybe—*"

"I'm in," I said.

I wasn't sure exactly *why* I said it, other than the fact that I couldn't quite stomach this particular ending to Seth's story. I didn't like the first ending, or the second one, but I'd accepted them. Just barely.

But both of those times, Seth had accepted them, too.

At least, I thought he did.

If that wasn't true... the least we could do was listen to whatever he had to say.

The guys all turned to look at me. Brody, Jesse, Zane and Dylan. Jesse's jaw flexed as he ground his teeth; he wasn't happy about what I was about to say. But I was going to say it anyway.

"I'm in... for having the conversation."

"Me too," Zane said. No hesitation. I couldn't really tell, though, if he was just "in" to irritate Jesse or if he really wanted Seth here.

Either way, the response was not good. Jesse glared at Zane like he was seriously considering throttling him. Brody turned and walked out.

He *walked out*.

Brody had never walked out on the band before. It was just a fucking *conversation*. Brody was our manager, and we counted on him for guidance.

But we all knew, when it came to anything to do with Jessa, Brody could be far less than reasonable.

"Anger management," Maggie said softly in his wake, in the strained silence. "He's... uh... working on it." She was sitting off to the side, quietly, listening to all of this, iPad gripped in her lap. Her knuckles looked painfully white.

So maybe she'd had something to do with Seth getting in here? If so, she was probably shitting herself right now.

Poor girl.

Zane kicked Dylan's boot. "Say something, man."

"I don't know." Dylan looked as exhausted as he sounded. "The guy almost tore us apart before. If it's already happening again, just over a conversation..."

"Seth Brothers is not tearing us apart," Jesse said firmly. "We're together on this. Aren't we?"

"Brody just walked out," Zane pointed out. He was poking the bear, probably still annoyed that Jesse wasn't seeing eye-to-eye with him about that teen guitar wiz.

"So you're gonna lose him to get Seth back?" Jesse accused Zane —and me. His dark gaze slammed into mine again.

"No one said that," Zane said, lounging back in his seat. The more pissed off Jesse got, the cooler Zane would get. It was a recipe for a fucking disaster. "And we're not losing Brody."

"You bring Seth back in here," Jesse retorted, "and we sure as fuck are."

"Brody will cool off." That was Maggie. She got to her feet. "And this doesn't have to be decided today. If there's a dialogue to be had about Seth—"

"If any of you actually think I'm *ever* getting in the same room with Seth Brothers again without talking to my sister first," Jesse said, steam-rolling right over Maggie, "you're dead fucking wrong. She should be here for this conversation."

This time, when he glared at me, I agreed, "Yes, she should."

Jesse stared at me for a beat, like maybe he'd expected me to argue. Then he got up and stalked out. As he went, his jeans brushed against mine, and I caught a whiff of his scent. Leather and cinnamon and gorgeous man, along with something that was vaguely Katie; sweet and vanilla.

I exhaled.

"Well, the auditions went well," Zane said.

Next to me, Dylan growled out a load of tension. "I'm so fucking tired of this shit," he bitched, rubbing his hands over his face.

Yeah. Me, too. But it wasn't like Dylan to lose his patience.

This was just plain *bad*.

"You really want Seth back?" he asked Zane.

"Fucking right," Zane said. "I wish we never lost him."

"You've all been here a long time." Maggie intervened, maybe sensing she needed to shut Zane up. She was pretty good at knowing when that time had come. "Let's just call it a day. I'll talk to Brody and we'll do whatever we need to do to find the right person."

"Thanks, Maggie," I said, when the guys just sat there in dark silence.

Maggie nodded, then turned and quietly let herself out. Zane got up to follow, but stopped to clasp hands with Dylan. "See you later?"

"Yeah," Dylan said. "I'll come by."

Then Zane turned to me. He moved in for a hug, so I got up to meet him. We embraced, but I wasn't exactly looking him in the eye when he asked, "You coming tonight?"

No, I wasn't coming. Was kinda hoping I wouldn't have to say so to his face, though.

Zane was throwing a belated birthday party for Woo at his place tonight. In reality, it was probably also a *Thank-fuck-we're-done-with-these-auditions* party. But now, maybe we weren't done. And I was still going to Kauai—the split second I walked out of here.

Zane held me out at arm's length. He was staring at me, and when I hesitated too long to answer him, he accused, "You ghosting?"

"Yes," I said, because what else could I say?

His hands dropped away. "What the fuck, Elle?"

"I'm done. For now."

"What the fuck does that mean?"

"It means I'm *done*. Taking a break. You all should too." I glanced down at Dylan, who was still sprawled back in his chair, tapping a drumstick against his skull and looking like he'd rather be having a root canal right now.

"Tell that to Brody and Maggie," Zane said.

"I have. They'll need time to work out the details with the network anyway. Extend shooting or whatever. Meanwhile, we can all take a breather."

Zane stared me down, but he didn't argue any further. We all knew this process was taking a toll, and I really didn't care what he thought about me jetting off to Kauai. I was supposed to have this break months ago, but this never ending search for a new guitarist kept postponing it.

How many times had he bailed on the band over the years because he had something more important to do, like get drunk, or get sober, or get laid?

This was my mental health we were talking about. We'd been working on the new album and searching for a new guitarist nonstop for a year while I also worked on about nine hundred other projects. I was officially overworked, overstressed and over the bullshit between Jesse and Zane—not to mention the bullshit between Jesse and me. If I didn't get some time away, I was gonna flip out, and it would not be pretty. Maggie and Joanie had been working, hard, to clear my schedule—a small miracle—and if Zane had a problem with me taking off, he could take it up with Brody. I was gone, and Zane could kiss my ass as I walked away.

But I bit that all back. Just barely.

He knew it, too. Those ice-blue eyes of his narrowed at me, a grin twitching at the corners of his mouth.

I smiled, grudgingly.

"Hope you find some hot dick in Hawaii," he said. "And cheer the fuck up."

My smile fell. He should talk; I wasn't the one who used sex to make myself feel better.

Although, these past seven months... that's exactly what I'd been doing. With Ash.

Zane didn't know about that, though. At least, I was pretty sure he didn't.

Either way, I probably should've been relieved. *This* was what everyone had wanted, ever since Jesse and I broke up, almost a year-and-a-half ago: for life in the band to go back to normal. And Zane used to talk to me like this—crudely—all the time. Since the breakup, though, he'd very conspicuously bit his tongue about my personal life.

It seemed the moratorium on that subject was finally over.

He smirked, because Zane loved having the last word, then turned and sauntered away.

"Hope you don't accidentally screw any underage chicks at your party tonight and end up in jail," I told his retreating back. "We're gonna need you on the tour."

He raised a fist and flipped his middle finger at me, then disappeared through the door.

Yeah. Back to normal enough.

I just stood here for a moment and sighed. I was officially *off*, and it was long past time. The crew was starting to reappear, discreetly tearing down equipment and packing out around me. I was off the hook. This thing was done—for now.

So why was I still standing here?

"How about you?"

I glanced down at Dylan. I'd kinda forgotten he was still here. "What?"

"Do you wish we never lost Seth?" he asked me.

I sighed again, a heavy, ragged sigh that came from somewhere deep inside. Somewhere wounded and so full of regret, I'd never been able to find the bottom of it. A place where I kept the two worst memories of my life: finding my friend unconscious, limp and pale, in a pool of his own vomit and blood... and a month later, turning my back on him.

"It doesn't matter," I said, my voice sounding small in the huge room. "It's not the same thing anyway. Sometimes I still wish I never lost Jesse, but that doesn't mean I want him back."

When I met Dylan's gaze, his green eyes were soft, his handsome face strained with worry. I couldn't remember a time when Dylan had ever been in the middle of any kind of drama between any of us—Zane, Jesse, me. It was always the three of us raising a shit storm, and Dylan, the calm in the eye of the cyclone.

I bent to kiss him, lightly, on the cheek. "I'll see you," I promised him.

But as I walked out, I really didn't know when that would be.

CHAPTER FIVE

Elle

BACKSTAGE WAS A TOTAL CLUSTERFUCK. Everyone was hurrying around, the production crew loading out and everyone else scrambling to get the hell out of the way of the band because, apparently, they'd all heard what happened in there and probably expected us to be breaking shit on our way out.

I saw Zane talking to Jude and Brody, but I didn't go near them. Maggie and Liv and Joanie all converged on me as I was beelining down the hall, but I shut them down with a raised hand.

"No one gets in," I told Joanie, and disappeared into my dressing room.

It was a storage room with metal shelving that housed bar stock —drink mixes and jars of olives—but they'd made it work for me, shoving everything up against the walls and bringing in a dressing table with a full-length mirror, portable lights, and a couple of wardrobe racks. I dropped into the chair at the table with a sigh. God, I just needed a minute alone to—

The door opened and Ash stepped in. I spun around to face him, but before I could get my mouth open, Joanie popped her head in behind him. "I... uh... assumed you didn't mean Ash."

Ash raised an eyebrow at me and I managed a half-smile. "It's okay," I told her, though it wasn't. Just because Joanie had figured out that I was screwing Ash—on occasion—didn't mean he got access to the inner sanctum anytime he felt like it.

I'd have to talk to her about it. Later.

She left, shutting the door and leaving me alone with Ash. When I met his eyes, he gave me an expectant look.

It was a look he'd been giving me a lot lately.

"How'd it go?" he asked.

I assumed he was being sarcastic, since he'd been in the room until Brody kicked everyone out; he'd been there when Seth got bounced.

"Awesome," I said, equally sarcastic.

He came over and reached for me, drawing me up out of the chair. "I know you guys are struggling to find someone, but you'll find someone. And, hey, if nothing works out..." He slipped his arms around me, gathering me close. "You can always hire me." He hit me with his charming smile, and I felt myself stiffen.

It wasn't the first time he'd said that.

The last few months, Ash had started dropping hints—at least, to me—about joining Dirty. And it wasn't that he wasn't talented enough. But in the past, we'd never even considered Ash, since he had his own band. He was lead singer of the Penny Pushers, and while the Pushers weren't as big as Dirty, they'd been together a long time and Ash was their frontman. It never occurred to us that he'd actually consider leaving them to play rhythm guitar with us.

The thing was, now that I was sleeping with him, I'd *never* agree to let him join Dirty.

But how could I tell him that?

I just hoped and prayed he didn't take the idea to Dylan. Because if Dylan got all excited about it and brought it to the band that Ash wanted in, and I said no, it would just get awkward. Everyone would demand to know *why* I was saying no.

And then I'd have to say something stupid, in front of everyone —in front of Jesse—about how I'd started sleeping with Ash to make myself feel better, when Jesse married Katie, even though I had no intention of actually being his girl... and now he was sniffing around to make me his girl... and he could never join Dirty because of my horny impulses.

Fucking embarrassing.

Not to mention everyone might be pissed at me for ruining our shot at an actually brilliant option for our new guitarist.

I could only hope Ash had thought that all through and planned to keep his mouth shut about it.

"Ash..." I started, not even sure what to say. How could I tell him not to say anything to the guys, not to ever ask them if he could join the band? He'd get mad. I knew that now. He'd take it as an insult; professional *and* personal rejection. Because for a while now, Ash had been trying to turn this thing between us into something it wasn't.

At least, for *me* it wasn't.

"Babe," he said, his blue eyes searching mine and his hands sliding down my back, "I'm just kidding."

But just like when he'd first offered to sleep with me to help me get over Jesse—*Friends with benefits*, he'd said—we both knew he wasn't kidding.

His hands slid down over my ass and squeezed gently. Then he moved in for a kiss, and I let him. He brushed his lips against mine, and when I closed my eyes, he tilted his head and went in deeper. The kiss was warm and demanding, and I sighed softly as his tongue slid between my lips.

Then his tongue piercing swept over my tongue, and I felt tingles at the back of my neck. Not the kind of sweeping, all-over tingles I'd felt the first time he kissed me—in the dark, out in the woods, the night of Jesse's wedding—but still... for a moment, I gave in to it. I was only female, after all.

And Ash was just so... *hot*.

He was the only man I'd had sex with in a long, long time... and it just so happened that he was really, really good at kissing.

And fucking.

As I kissed him back, he groaned and gripped my hips, pulling me against him and pressing his solid length against me; his cock, hard and eager in his jeans, jabbed against my groin. I felt the answering surge of lust in my own body, deep in my belly, between my legs. And for the first time ever, it felt off-putting. Alarming, somehow.

Uncomfortable.

I pulled away.

He tried to kiss me again, but I dodged, twisting out of his grip. His hands fell away. His blue eyes were hazed up with desire, but there was concern there, too.

"You okay?"

"No," I said. "I'm not okay. Seth just *auditioned* to join Dirty."

He shoved his hands in his back pockets and looked weirdly guilty. "Yeah."

I crossed my arms and drew back, studying him, as it dawned on me; I didn't think he could see the guitarists auditioning beyond the screen, but... "Did you know it was him up there?"

"Yeah."

"You could've said something."

He raised an eyebrow, slightly. "You pissed at me?"

"No. Of course not." Though I kind of was. Unjustly.

He looked around the room at my things, like they'd somehow tell him something I wasn't saying. He glanced at my giant Givenchy tote purse, the one I always traveled with. "You still going to Hawaii?"

"Yes." Why wouldn't I be going?

"You know..." he said, still looking around, suddenly fascinated with a trash can in the corner, "... I have a couple of days before I have to be back in Vancouver."

Oh, God. *Please, don't say it...*

"I could come with you."

"Oh."

He lifted his blue eyes to meet mine.

"I just... I need some time with Joanie, Ash. I told her... we're going to go over my schedule and get organized, and..." I trailed off, because as much as Ash might be trying to kid himself there was more between us than there really was, he wasn't dense. All I'd talked about for months was how badly I needed some time off, and now I was making excuses about Joanie and I needing time to work?

But it just didn't seem cool to say, *I need some time to lay around on the beach in a bikini and drink cocktails, and I don't want to do that with you.*

"Okay," he said, his eyes tightening a bit. He knew I was making excuses. "You wanna grab some dinner before you go?"

"No. Thanks. I already ate a bit. And I'll eat on the way."

"You're pissed at me," he said. This time, it wasn't a question.

"I don't know," I said, my agitation with both him and myself growing. "You should've said something, Ash."

"Why? You wouldn't have let him play?"

"I don't know. But it's not your call."

"No. It was Liv's call. But if it was up to me, I'd let him play."

"Ash—"

"He's *Seth Brothers*," he said, as if I didn't know.

I turned away.

I didn't expect him to understand. I didn't expect anyone to understand, really.

No one else was there when Brody alluded to what happened between Seth and Jessa. Just the band, Jude and Maggie. We'd never said, publicly, why Seth was dismissed from the band—again.

The truth was, we didn't really *know*. Brody and Jesse had more or less decided it was so, and no one else really wanted to argue with Brody or Jesse when it came to Jessa. Dylan didn't have that kind of fight in him, and at the time, I didn't have it in me to challenge Jesse. I could barely be in a room with him if we weren't playing music. Whenever the music stopped, I was gone. I'd only recently begun to hang around for any more than that, and mostly because of my contractual obligation to the documentary series.

Zane had tried to argue, at first, but it was clear Jesse wasn't having it. He wasn't having Seth in the band anymore. And from the look on Brody's face when he'd attacked Seth at the church, Seth had been lucky he'd only been fired, and not worse.

I really would've killed him...

That's what Brody said as I held him, bleeding, just before he puked and passed out from the concussion he'd gotten, hitting his head on an amp while he and Seth struggled.

So much *animosity*. Over Jessa.

And I still didn't understand *why*.

I'd asked Jessa myself, a few months ago. After the dust had seemed to settle and she and Brody were all blissed out on being in love, I'd asked her point blank if she'd asked Brody and Jesse to kick Seth out of the band—and she said no. She told me, actually, that she felt bad Seth had cleared out without any kind of fight.

Which made two of us.

And I knew for a fact, as of today, that Zane would agree.

So why were Brody and Jesse still dead set against Seth, as if they were protecting her from him?

"Hey." Ash slipped his hands around my waist and pressed up against my backside. "I'm sorry. Maybe whatever's going on between you guys and Seth is worse than I thought. I guess when I saw him backstage, I just got excited. Like if he had the balls to show up here he must really want back with the band, and maybe you guys would want to see that. I don't know." He kissed my neck and I pulled away without even thinking about it. I turned to him.

"Ash... I really can't talk about this right now."

It was true, but mostly I just couldn't talk about this with *him*. It was Dirty stuff, and Ash wasn't part of Dirty.

Thanks to me, he never would be, and that just made me feel shitty. Because if anyone had told me, back *before* I got naked with him, that Ash was willing to leave the Pushers for Dirty, I might've been thrilled.

"Can you just give me some space on this?" I asked him. I could barely look at him, much less take his kisses like I deserved them right now. Not only did I feel shitty about—quite literally—screwing him out of a chance to join Dirty, I felt even shittier about what just happened with Seth. Ash was right. If he had the balls to show up here he must *really* want back with the band.

And why would he do that if he felt the least bit guilty about whatever happened between him and Jessa in the past?

"Sure." Ash said. "Of course." He was still hovering, though. "You want me to wait for you outside?"

"No, thanks. I don't know how long I'll be. I need to talk to the guys."

And with that, Ash went silent. It was a dark, cold silence.

Then: "Jesse already left. With Katie."

And there it was.

Ash was always here to remind me, in any way possible, that Jesse was with his wife. As if he was making sure I wasn't going to do anything stupid—like fall for Jesse again.

"Ash... I just need some time, okay?"

He nodded, grudgingly. He took a step toward me, but it was hesitant. He kept staring at me like he was waiting for me to say something else, but I didn't.

Then he leaned in and kissed me softly on the lips. "Call me when you land? So I know you're okay."

"Sure."

I watched him leave, then exhaled. When did we get here? Ash, worrying about me? Wanting me to call him when I got wherever I was going and check in?

I gathered my small personal items from the room, some makeup and my phone, and shoved them into my tote. Joanie would arrange for the rest—clothes and shoes, and flowers people had sent for me—to be packed up and taken to my house. At least Ash hadn't sent flowers; they were from my publicist and the record company and my girlfriend, Summer.

I waited a few minutes to be sure Ash had cleared out before emerging from the room, all the while wondering, when did we get *here*? Me, hiding out, to avoid Ash?

God. What a shit show.

I knew I was gonna have to deal with him. He was starting to act like a possessive boyfriend, when I didn't particularly *want* a boyfriend.

And even if I did... I definitely didn't want him to be Ashley Player.

Ash was great—as a friend. And as a friend with benefits—yeah. He was super fucking hot. He definitely knew what to do with his pierced tongue *and* his pierced dick.

He was not, however, boyfriend material.

Though I probably should've thought of that *before* I fucked him.

It wasn't like I didn't know, from the very start, that this whole "friends with benefits" deal was a bad idea.

CHAPTER SIX

Elle

I FOUND Brody in the hallway, alone, talking on his phone. As I approached, I heard him say, "I'll call you in a bit... 'Bye, baby." Which meant he was talking to Jessa.

Jesse's sister was officially part of Dirty again; we'd contracted her as a songwriter. But she wasn't part of the audition process. She was home in Vancouver right now, which meant Brody was calling her every chance he got to check in and keep her updated. Because that's what people did when they were a *couple*.

In what world did "friends with benefits" need to check in?

I tried to just let my irritation over the conversation with Ash roll off. Right now, I needed all my irritation for Brody.

"Well that was bullshit," I told him, when he looked up and saw me coming.

"Which part?" he asked flatly. Clearly he was as unimpressed as I was with what went down in that audition—just for different reasons.

"You," I said bluntly. "Walking out."

"You know I'm not gonna do anything to upset Jessa right now," he said. And yes, I knew that.

And no, I didn't blame him for it.

But that still didn't make what had happened in there okay.

"Brody, you've always been honest with me. When Jesse wasn't... you know, happy, when we were together... you were the only one who was truly, painfully honest with me. So I'm asking you to dig deep and be honest with me now." I took a breath and asked him: "Do you really believe Seth did something out of line with Jessa?"

I wasn't going to say the word *rape*. I just couldn't.

I'd never been able to reconcile that word with Seth and Jessa in my head.

Months ago, long after Brody had spat that word in Seth's face, when I'd asked Jessa if she'd *wanted* Seth fired and she'd admitted to me that she didn't, I'd decided that "rape" was most likely an incredibly inflammatory word for whatever had actually happened between the two of them, selected by Brody's male ego, to sum up his personal feelings about the matter.

I'd never shared that theory with anyone.

But he knew what I was asking.

He said nothing, his deep blue eyes fixed on me, and his face, well... I could tell he was struggling *not* to be pissed at me. So that was something.

"I mean," I pushed on, "other than just be a stupid, lonely kid who took too many drugs and maybe fell in love?"

"I don't wanna hear about it, Elle," he said quietly. Too quietly.

"Too bad. He was an *orphan*, Brody—"

"You can save the poor lonely orphan story, Elle. I've heard it all before. From Jessa. And what he was was a grown-ass *man*."

"He was nineteen," I fired back. "And he was an orphan. And an addict. And we were all he had."

"Where the fuck is this coming from?" Brody demanded, more than a little venom in his voice, and it took me aback. Brody had never talked to me like this, but of course, when it came to Jessa, the man was an overprotective bear. Always had been.

"It's coming from my *gut*," I said. "Because I didn't see a guilty man on that stage today. Did you?"

Brody's chest rose as he drew a deep, incredibly slow breath—maybe part of his anger management therapy. Then he said, quietly, "Jessa's part of Dirty, Elle. She's got a contract. Unless that changes, I don't see Seth fitting in, do you?"

I didn't have an answer for that. I wasn't about to stand here and speak for Jessa, like he was. But I meant what I'd said.

Why would a guilty man come back, and get up on that stage, in front of all of us, in front of the cameras, in front of the world, just to play his heart out for us and risk rejection all over again?

Risk another broken nose, or worse?

I turned on my heel and walked away.

"Let me know when you're coming back from Kauai," Brody said behind me, but I didn't even answer. I hadn't yet told anyone exactly when I'd be back, for a reason. I didn't *know* when I'd be back.

Right now, I felt no obligation to be anywhere other than on that beach. My only pressing commitment was to Dirty, finding a guitarist and finishing the album, which had been put on hold, again, while we filmed this thing. I'd come back for that when I was needed.

Until then, I was on vacation.

On my way out, there was one more person I hoped to see, though. I knew Jude had to have let Seth into the bar, because no one got past Jude and his team.

But no one knew where he was.

I told Joanie I was ready to leave, and on our way out, Flynn appeared. A longtime member of our security team, Flynn had been "promoted" this year—assigned to me, as my personal bodyguard and driver; ever since my solo album launched me into an even higher level of the megastardom stratosphere a few years back, Jude no longer let me go anywhere without one.

The three of us, Flynn, Joanie and I, headed out back. Jude's bike was still here, but he was nowhere to be seen, and I wasn't going back inside to look for him.

I'd just have to talk to him later.

Liv was outside, her crew loading equipment into a couple of giant trucks. "Elle," she said, falling into step with me. I didn't even stop. "Can I ask you about Seth? On-camera?"

"Not right now." That was my polite way of saying *Not ever*.

"Just a teeny, tiny soundbite?" she pressed. "Something. Anything? I need a reaction from *someone* in the band. Just a few words?"

"She said not now." That was Flynn. Somehow, he managed to angle his broad shoulders in-between us and stop Liv in her tracks as I slipped into the SUV with Joanie.

"Sorry, Liv," I said, again to be polite. I wasn't sorry.

I was accustomed to cameras, but I was done with this whole documentary experience. Cameras and crew in my face all day, every day for the last three weeks. First, interviews with all of us, then behind-the-scenes stuff with the band, playing at the church, doing what we do on a daily basis. They'd filmed me working out, getting my hair and makeup done, eating lunch with Dylan—as if that was somehow interesting?—whatever they could get. Then the two straight weeks of auditions, with insanely long hours every day.

I liked Liv, but I'd had enough.

Flynn shut my door and went around to the driver's seat.

"Don't worry about Liv," Joanie said supportively. "We'll schedule another interview, if and when you're ready. If not, I'll talk to Brody."

That had become her mantra of late.

I'll talk to Brody.

I'll talk to Jesse.

She'd even gone so far as to step up with *I'll talk to Zane.*

The woman was fearless. She took her job seriously and she'd come through for me, big time, since the breakup with Jesse. Taken it upon herself to deal with shit she really didn't need to, just so I didn't have to.

These days, I didn't know what the hell I'd do without her.

"It'll be fine," I told her as we pulled out, a statement that was neither here nor there. Did I want her to fight my battles with Brody for me?

No.

Would I let her?

Possibly, yes.

I sighed and sank into my seat, trying not to look at Liv standing there in the lot, watching me drive away. I could feel the question in her eyes, following me: *What are you all hiding?*

What are you so afraid of?

Liv really missed her calling as an investigative journalist.

"Do you want to go over things now?" Joanie offered, probably trying to distract me.

"In a minute. Just make sure my schedule is totally cleared for the next few days. Like, I want to owe nothing, and to no one." *One could only dream.*

Talented as she was, though, Joanie wasn't a miracle worker.

"You want me to reschedule the call with Danielle?"

Shit. Danielle. I'd forgotten I was supposed to have an important conference call with my publicist and her team.

"That's Monday?"

"It's tomorrow," Joanie said. "But I can get it moved."

A bold offer, since Danielle had been all over me the last few weeks about this meeting. We had a lot to talk about with the upcoming *Kiss & Tell* campaign; my new lipstick line was launching in two months. She was not gonna be happy to hear from Joanie on this instead of me.

"Move it to next week," I said. "I need seven days. Just get me seven days and I'll love you forever."

"You already love me forever," she said.

"I really, really do." I put my head back on the seat. "Music. Please."

Joanie tapped her phone, and through the wonders of Bluetooth, Lenny Kravitz's "Always on the Run" filled the air. Joanie had everything I'd ever want to hear at her fingertips; she was that good to me. I should've been thinking about giving her another raise. As soon as I was back from vacay...

As we slid to a stop at a red light, I rolled my head to gaze out the tinted window. And I saw him there.

It was pretty dark out... but it was definitely him.

Sitting on the curb in front of the taco place across from the bar. He was leaned back against the drive-thru sign, like some street busker, but his guitar case, discarded next to him, wasn't open for change. The dirty old man sitting next to him—and he was literally dirty—was holding his acoustic, and the two of them were chatting.

"Fuck me." I sat up.

The old man was obviously homeless. But despite his faded T-shirt and the rips in his jeans, Seth Brothers was far from that.

Wasn't he?

Jesus, what was he doing? Hanging out on the curb like yesterday's trash...?

Was he scoring drugs?

The thought passed through my mind, far too disturbing to ponder for any length of time.

"Stop. Pull over!" I called up to Flynn as we started to drive off. "Can you pull around? To the taco place."

"You want drive-thru?" Flynn asked; I never ate fast food. But he threw on his turn signal and squeezed into the turning lane.

"Just pull into the lot," I said.

He did. He pulled around into one of the narrow spots along the side of the taco place and I immediately hopped out. Flynn got out behind me to stand guard, because that's what Flynn did, even if I was just buying a taco.

But I walked right past the door of the restaurant and over to Seth. The old homeless man was twiddling on the guitar; they were talking about music, as far as I could tell. The old man looked up at me first. When he saw me standing over them, his eyes widened in his heavily-lined face.

Then Seth looked up, too.

"I want to talk to you," I said.

I did. As soon as I saw him sitting here on the curb... I just had to.

"This your girl?" the old man asked, smiling. His words were slurry. He sounded drunk, maybe, or unwell. Or it could've just been his age and the missing teeth.

"No," Seth said. He was looking up at me with caution. Confusion. Wondering what the fuck I was doing here, probably. But his tone was calm and level when he said, "This is Elle."

"Elle," the old man repeated, savoring the sound of my name. "Pretty name for a pretty girl."

"Thank you," I said.

"Looks like I've gotta go, Gus," Seth told the old man, but his eyes were still on me.

"Sometimes the angels come a-callin'," the old man mused, handing over Seth's guitar. "Be a fool of a man to pass 'em up."

Seth packed his acoustic away and got to his feet. He was still looking at me when he said, "Isn't that the truth."

"I'm no angel," I told the old man, mostly because I felt uncomfortable looking Seth in the eye. He was mere feet away from me, and I wasn't ready for that.

"Look like one to me," the old man said, still smiling his gummy smile at me.

I turned and walked back to the SUV. Flynn met me halfway, or rather, he intercepted Seth.

"Where's he going?"

I stifled the urge to roll my eyes. "You can pat him down if you want to," I said. "I'm sure he won't mind."

I wasn't sure of that, but I wanted Flynn to feel ridiculous for thinking it.

He looked Seth over, but let it drop. As I gestured for Joanie to vacate the back seat, he took Seth's guitar cases from him without a word and loaded them into the back of the truck. Joanie slipped out and hurried up to the front, and we—Seth and I—got into the back.

"Where to?" Flynn asked me as he settled into the driver's seat.

"The airport," I answered, because nothing had changed. I was sleeping in Kauai tonight, and nothing was getting in the way of that.

After a brief hesitation, during which I assumed Flynn was considering saying more—but wisely chose not to—he started up the truck and got us on our way.

"You want music?" Joanie asked from the front. Translation: *Should I put the music back on so it's harder for us to eavesdrop?*

"Yes," I said, and she cranked up Lenny.

After a tense few blocks, I managed to look over at Seth.

He was sitting there looking uncomfortable and somehow laid-back at the same time. His eyes met mine instantly, and I saw the trepidation there. He had no idea what this was.

Neither did I, just yet.

"What were you doing?" I asked him, much more contempt in my voice than was warranted. "Busking?"

"I was talking to Gus," he said evenly. "He was teaching me a song."

"He was teaching *you*?"

"He had a band back in the day. Played the blues."

"Oh."

Well, that was lovely. A glimpse of where Seth might've ended up if he hadn't gotten clean, maybe. I wasn't even sure why that made me so damn uncomfortable. Guilt?

"You have a lot of friends on the street?"

"Some," he said, seemingly unfazed by that concept.

I let it drop. But I kept looking at him, even when he looked away.

When he was onstage in the bar, I hadn't gotten a very good look. The screen wasn't out of the way for long, and I was so shocked, not to mention distracted by the tension in the room and the reactions of everyone else, that I hadn't fully absorbed what I was seeing.

He looked good. Really good.

Healthy.

And the shorter hair suited him.

He'd taken his shades off, and his eyes met mine again. Those were the same as ever. A pale, smoky green, almost grayish, with gold around the pupils. But there was something in them I couldn't put my finger on. Something new. A self-assurance, maybe. A maturity.

But just like when I saw him onstage tonight... I did not see a guilty man looking back at me.

"I'm listening," he said. "Whatever you have to say, you can say it."

"Not yet," I said. And I told him, "I'm still pissed at you."

I really was.

There was a whole shitload of conflicting feelings swirling through me right now, some of them ugly, but I knew better than to let them all come spilling out. First, I needed a little time to gather my thoughts so I wouldn't explode in anger. Or guilt—which was anger at myself.

He didn't flinch, didn't even blink when he said, "I know."

I tore my eyes away and dug my phone out of my purse, mostly because I wanted him to think I had something else I needed to do. Though all I really needed to do right now was scrape my head together. It was an impulse, picking him up. But I didn't regret it. I just couldn't stand the sight of him sitting there on the street.

Guilt, yes. But something else, too.

It was *wrong*.

Seth had been my friend once. A good friend. A *true* friend.

Over the years, I'd definitely come to learn the value of a true friend. They were fucking invaluable.

How could I just drive on by, like Seth never meant anything to me at all?

I couldn't. Maybe Brody could. Maybe the guys in the band could.

I could not.

When I checked my phone, I already had texts from Jesse, Ash,

Maggie and Liv, but I ignored them all. Joanie had also texted me, from the front seat.

Joanie: Everything ok?

I texted her back a quick *Yes*. Because everything was okay. At least, with our travel plans.

I still could not wait to get out of here.

I was still weary as fuck of all the stand-offs. Jesse and Zane, locking horns over every guitarist we auditioned—Seth included. And now Brody was so pissed he'd walked out on the band. Maggie and Zane didn't even seem to be talking to each other lately, and I wasn't even sure if anyone else had noticed, or if it was just me. I knew I should check in with her about that, see if everything was okay, let her know she could talk to me. God knew she'd refereed Zane's battles with everyone else; if she was having issues with him herself, someone should step up.

But I was just so fucking weary of it all.

I really needed this break.

Not only did I not know what to say to Seth right now, I didn't have the energy to say it. To deal with whatever he might say back... or what everyone else was gonna say when they found out that I— gasp of horror—gave Seth a *ride* somewhere and had a *conversation* with him.

It was all starting to border on fucking juvenile.

And anyway, even if I'd had the energy to deal with it all, I did not have the time. Not today.

So I turned to him again and said the only thing that seemed reasonable to say.

"Do you have plans tonight?"

CHAPTER SEVEN

Seth

I STARED AT ELLE... sitting there with her platinum hair and her flawless makeup, looking back at me with her steel-gray eyes. I wasn't even sure what she was asking me, exactly.

My only plan tonight—and for the last many years of my life—had been to reunite with Dirty. And since that clearly wasn't happening today... Yeah. I was pretty fucking wide open.

"No plans," I said.

"Good. Then you can come to Hawaii."

"Hawaii?"

"Kauai." She wasn't looking at me anymore, just watching traffic roll by out her window. "Have you ever been?"

"No."

"It's the best island. You'll like it. Woo has a place there where I sometimes stay. I'm on my way there now."

"Right now?"

She looked over at me. "Now."

I just stared at her some more.

Why the hell was Elle inviting me to Hawaii?

"What is this...?" I asked her.

"It's an olive branch," she said. "The flight's on me. What you do when you get there is up to you. You can stay at Woo's with me and Joanie, if you want to. We'll have security," she added, pausing for effect, and the warning wasn't lost on me. "But I can't make you stay and talk to me. This isn't a kidnapping. And I'm not promising you anything with the band. This isn't about the band. I don't speak for Dirty. This is just me, saying I'm sorry to an old friend and I wish things didn't go down the way they did but they did... and I want you to be okay."

I had no idea what to say to that.

This was the only apology of any kind I'd ever gotten from anyone in the band. Not that I expected any. They were justified in firing me. At least, the first time.

Was she apologizing for that? Or the second firing?

Or both?

She turned to look out the window again. "This is all I can do right now to make sure you're okay. It's a moment. I'm feeling generous. Just take it."

So I took it.

"Okay," I said. "I'll come."

She looked at me again, her gray eyes hard and direct. "And Seth, if there are any drugs..." She trailed off for a moment. Then she finished: "I'm so gone from your life, you'll never get near me again."

"Understood."

She looked away and fell silent, and she didn't say another word to me on the drive to the airport.

I didn't push it.

I didn't really give a fuck about Hawaii. But *this*... it was something I'd fucking dreamed of.

Well... I'd definitely never dreamed of Elle inviting me to fly to Hawaii with her. That was so far beyond the realms of what I'd ever thought was possible, I'd never bothered to have those kinds of dreams. But I'd definitely wanted this for so fucking long, I couldn't remember what it was like *not* to want this. Elle. Zane. Jesse. Dylan. Any one of them, actually wanting to talk to me.

I'd be stupid as fuck to pass up the opportunity to make amends with anyone in the band. But despite her apology, I still wasn't quite sure if that was what was happening here or not.

All I knew for absolute sure—and I knew that Elle knew it, too—was that the rest of the band, and Brody, were not gonna be happy about this.

I was doing it anyway.

And for some reason that was completely beyond me, so was she.

🎸

The flight to Lihue Airport was just over six hours, on a luxury chartered jet, and there were only four people in the giant cabin. Me, Elle, her assistant, Joanie, and her bodyguard, who'd grudgingly introduced himself to me as Flynn. Five people, if you counted the flight attendant ghosting in and out.

The four of us sat in opposite corners of the cabin, and there was very little conversation.

Joanie slept most of the flight. Flynn read magazines and didn't say a word.

Mostly I just played my acoustic, quietly.

Elle was on her laptop, ear buds in, and rarely lifted her eyes from her screen. I had no idea if she was working or what. But she didn't speak to me.

As soon as we landed, she was on her phone. Flynn got us a rental car, a luxury SUV, and piled everyone's bags in back. I had no bag, just my guitars, because I wasn't exactly gonna ask them to detour into Santa Monica so I could collect my shit from Lauren's place. Flynn got in behind the wheel, Joanie was up front, and Elle, beside me in the back, was still on her phone.

"I don't know, Ash. I'll let you know when I'm back," she said. "I don't *know*. We can talk about it later, okay?" She sounded irritated, anxious to get off the phone. Ash didn't let her off, though, for another few minutes of semi-arguing.

It was the dead of night. Los Angeles was two hours ahead of us, but still. I had no idea if Ash knew Elle was here with me, but she definitely didn't bring it up.

When she got off the phone, she sighed softly, stuffed her phone in her purse, and lay her head back on the seat.

Within a few minutes, her head lolled against the window. She was asleep.

Forty-five minutes later, as we rolled up Woo's winding, tree-lined driveway, sparkling with lanterns in the night, I was still studying her. Trying to figure her out.

To figure out what she was really doing here with *me*.

I'd heard her on the phone with Ash, and it wasn't the kind of conversation friends have. Obviously there was something going on there. And I'd seen the way men looked at her. Men at the airport. Our pilot. Even Flynn.

It wasn't just that she was gorgeous. Beyond her looks, Elle had always had that *something* about her; she just wasn't your ordinary girl. She carried herself in a way you could feel across a room. Literally, heads turned for her.

She was a star, in every sense of the word.

And I wondered where that bright, sassy, but down-to-Earth girl I used to know had gone.

I could still see her, sitting there, just an arm's length from me. Under the designer clothing and the makeup. I saw her, living this massive, glamorous life, just like it was second nature to her, yet she didn't seem comfortable in the middle of it. More like... practiced. Like she'd learned to live with it.

I saw how she wore it, like a tailor-made dress, one she'd forgotten how to take off at the end of the day. Her cool detachment from it all. Her aloneness in the middle of her own life.

The most famous member of Dirty...

I shouldn't have been able to get near *her*, of all people, but for some reason, she'd let me in. At least this far.

She was the only member of Dirty who'd extended the olive branch to me.

And I could not figure out why.

"Bella will set you up in one of the guest cottages," Elle said, as she introduced me to Woo's housekeeper. We were standing in his enormous kitchen, one wall of floor-to-ceiling windows standing open to the night. It smelled of freshly-brewed coffee and flowers and the ocean. I could hear the waves crashing on the shore beyond the yard, below the rocky cliffs.

"It's all ready for you," Bella said, smiling up at me. She was a tiny, lively sixty-something. "I can show you the way, if you like."

I glanced at Elle, who stood back, watching me. She crossed her arms but said nothing. I noticed that Flynn and Joanie had vanished into the woodwork. Flynn had briefly scoped out the house before disappearing. I didn't even think Joanie had set foot inside.

There were four small but cozy-looking guest huts in the side yard, and all of us, except Elle, were sleeping in them. It was around four a.m., but I didn't feel much like sleeping.

"Thank you," I told Bella. "I can find it myself."

After a quick chat with Elle at the front door, Bella headed home. She'd waited up for us to arrive, and had insisted on giving me a tour of Woo's house when we did. In what would've been a den off the dining room, there was a full recording studio. The living room had a grand piano and high glass walls that looked out on the back yard, where there was a sprawling patio with a fire pit. The five bedrooms upstairs overlooked the tree-lined yard, rocky cliffs and the dark expanse of the ocean beyond.

The house was tucked away from the road, among the trees. Private and about as secluded as you could get around here.

All in all, I could see why Elle chose to come here.

She drifted back into the kitchen, where I was leaning on the island, looking out into the dark. I'd already poured myself a coffee.

"You want one?" I asked her, lifting my mug.

Her eyes met mine. She had her arms wrapped securely around herself, but she said, "Sure." She settled onto one of the cushioned window seats overlooking the back yard. I felt her eyes on me as I fixed her a coffee.

"You like cream? Sugar?"

"Just cream," she said.

I brought her mug to her. It had a little hula girl on it and said *I Got Lei'd in Waikiki*.

"Thanks." Her lips quirked a bit at the mug, but she didn't exactly smile. She took it and sipped. She was still looking at me, on and off, and since she hadn't told me to fuck off yet, I figured I'd just stick around until she did.

I took a seat in one of the cushioned chairs opposite her, facing out the window. She had her back to the dark now, facing me, with her legs pulled up on the window seat, her long, soft gray dress wrapped around them. She'd changed since we arrived. The dress had thin straps; one of them was almost falling off, her tanned shoulders bare and set squarely against me as she hugged her knees to her chest.

"So," she said. "Are you okay?" She looked and sounded guarded, but at least she was talking to me.

And I thought about what she might want to hear. About how loaded that question, and the various answers to it, might be.

"Most days," I said.

It was true enough. Ever since I got clean, my life had been a pretty steady stream of *okay*.

She nodded once, like she was squaring that away inside herself. Checking off a box somewhere in her head. Then she sipped her coffee and looked at her toes. Her nails were painted in gold glitter and she wiggled them, picking at the toe ring on her middle toe.

"How about you?" I asked her.

She looked up at me, her slim eyebrows squeezing together. "I'm fine."

"Yeah? How's life in the eye of the storm?"

She shrugged. "It's what it looks like."

"It looks exhausting."

"Yeah." She looked exhausted when she said, "It's that."

"Do you enjoy it? Everyone wanting a piece of you?" I held her steel gaze and added, "Loving you... Loving to hate you... Just waiting for you to fuck up." I knew, personally, that was my least favorite part of fame. But you couldn't take all the perks of success as a rock star without the rest of it.

She nodded, slowly. "You could say it's a real love-hate situation."

"Lonely?"

"What?"

"Is it lonely?" I asked her.

She looked baffled by the question. Caught off-guard. Maybe no one had ever really asked her that before. Her eyes narrowed at me a little and she frowned. "Why would it be lonely? I'm never alone."

I said nothing.

"How about you?" she asked. "How's Ray?"

I shrugged. "Same old Ray."

Ray Brothers was my foster father, for lack of a better term. A simple man, Ray liked simple things. His TV, his couch, and his lite beer. But he was a good man. Took me in at thirteen and took care of me for a few years, on and off—whenever I wasn't in juvie for getting caught dealing pot. Even after his wife died, he'd taken me in, until he injured his back at work and had to go on disability and the powers that be said he couldn't anymore.

He'd been the closest thing to an actual father figure in my life. My own father, Todd Becker—a man who'd bounced in and out of jail before bouncing right out of my life—definitely hadn't been. Ray had even offered me his last name when I turned nineteen. Said I could have it, if I wanted it. Said it could be a new start, a chance to start fresh on a life of my own and leave behind my crappy childhood.

I'd taken him up on the offer. At the time, I really thought it was a fresh start.

Little did I know that the worst times of my life were yet to come.

"Think he's waiting on me to visit," I added. "He doesn't like that I live so far away these days."

Elle cocked her head at me a little. "Where do you live?" she asked. And it felt so fucking strange, that she didn't even know the answer to that.

But why would she?

"L.A., sometimes. New York. Austin. Wherever."

"You have a place there? 'Wherever'?"

"Have a lot of places," I said. "None of my own, if that's what you mean. I kinda float around. Rolling stone gathers no moss, or some such shit?"

"And you like that? Floating around?"

"Mostly," I said.

"It doesn't get lonely?" Her steel-gray eyes held a challenge.

"I'm never alone," I said, repeating her own words.

"Uh-huh." She looked me over, carefully, like she was trying to read me. Or understand me. "You have a girlfriend?"

I shrugged. "There was a girl. Michelle. We had a thing on and off, last couple of years."

"And?"

"And she's in Boston. And I'm here."

"You're not together anymore?"

"We were never really together. Just... good friends."

"Friends." Elle considered that. "With benefits?"

"If you want to call it that."

She shook her head as she said, "I don't know, Seth... Boston seems like a long way to go for a booty call."

"Not if you live in Boston," I said.

"Oh." She went silent, maybe wondering when the hell I'd lived in Boston.

"Before that," I offered, "there was Lauren. She's in L.A.."

"Another friend?"

"Right. And before that... I was a junkie, and so was pretty much every girl I got involved with. The ones that weren't... well... once they see behind the curtain, it ain't so pretty, they don't last very long."

"But that was a long time ago."

Yeah; she was definitely challenging me. Feeling me out. Watching for any sign that I was gonna fuck up. Any sign that she needed to call Flynn in here to vacate my ass.

"Right," I said, holding her gaze. "A long time ago."

"Have you ever had a real relationship?" She sipped her coffee, watching me over the brim of her mug. "You know, since you got clean."

"What is that?" I asked her. "Flowers and walks on the beach?"

"Maybe? Those seem like pretty regular things to do with someone you care about."

"Then I guess I'm just not that regular," I said.

CHAPTER EIGHT

Seth

"AND WHAT ABOUT JESSA?" Elle asked me after a long, but not uncomfortable, silence.

She was still sitting in the window seat, still on guard, but as we'd sat in Woo's kitchen, talking, it felt like we were gaining ground. Millimeter by millimeter, maybe. And it seemed to me that the world outside was falling away. That nothing was more important than this conversation. Right here, right now.

Me. Elle.

Answering her questions and chipping away at the bullshit that time and hurt feelings and too many stupid mistakes had layered between us.

I had no idea, though, how to answer that particular question.

"What about Jessa?"

"She's with Brody now," she said, studying my reaction.

I didn't really have one. I'd accepted, long ago, that Jessa Mayes wasn't mine. That she'd never loved me the way I hoped she would. That her heart had always been out of my reach, because it belonged to someone else.

And the fact that she was with Brody didn't surprise me. It only surprised me that they weren't together from day one.

"Yeah," I said.

"It doesn't bother you?"

"Why would it bother me?"

"I don't know. You two dated."

"Yeah. I guess you could call it that."

"What would you call it?"

"Jessa and I had a relationship," I admitted, treading carefully. I had no idea what Elle knew, or believed, or how she felt about that relationship. "It wasn't exactly... conventional. We were both kind of... lost, back then." I didn't know how else to put it. "And it wasn't out in the open. But you know that now."

"We all know," Elle said. "But it's not like we didn't have a clue back then. At least, I did. I saw how you were with her. I just thought..." She trailed off, hugging her knees tighter. She looked down at her feet and picked at her nail polish. And it hit me, as I watched her face change—that Elle felt... guilty? For what happened between me and Jessa? "I just thought you had a crush on her."

"I can imagine," I said, carefully. "I can imagine what you saw."

"Brody didn't want to see it, I'm sure. But you did like her." She looked up at me. "And as far as I could tell, she liked you, too."

"Yeah, I liked her."

That Jessa liked me too, at some point, was beyond question. But how much and for how long, I really couldn't say.

"Always?" Elle asked me, her gray eyes searching my face.

"Not always," I said. "After a while. And until she wanted out. Or sometime thereafter." I shrugged. "I was young and more than a little dumb. It might've taken longer than it should've to get the message."

Elle's eyebrows twisted together. "I'm not particularly young, Seth," she said softly. "And I'm not dumb. But it took me a long, long time to get the message."

Jesse. She was talking about Jesse.

I did not know what to say. But it definitely wasn't lost on me that she'd just shared something incredibly personal with me.

"So... when did you get the message?" she asked.

I thought about that. It wasn't exactly clear to me, a specific moment in time, when I'd realized Jessa was done with me—and there wasn't a damn thing I could do about it. If it happened like that, I couldn't recall it.

"The last time I saw her, maybe. At that party at Brody's place. The break in the first tour."

"I remember that night," Elle said. "Great party."

Yeah. But not for me.

"Jessa and I had been at odds a while," I said. "We'd stopped sleeping together." I watched to see how she'd take that, but she showed no reaction. Her guard was still way up, her expression carefully neutral, but not neutral. I didn't know what it was; I didn't really know how to read Elle all that well. I probably never did. "I wanted to get back together with her but she told me she wouldn't. Said she was in love with Brody."

I'd been so hurt by her words, and so messed up by that point—and so fucked on coke—I'd called her a whore. I remembered that, vividly. I was so crushed over losing her, and I'd wanted to hurt her.

I was beyond caring, at that point, about hurting myself.

But I didn't mention any of that to Elle.

There were some things I was still too ashamed of to share with most people, and calling Jessa Mayes a whore for breaking up with me and being in love with Brody definitely qualified.

"Was that the worst it got?" Elle asked, her gaze on me steadfast.

"No," I admitted. "When she first broke things off with me, before that, it got pretty ugly. It was just before we wrote 'Dirty Like Me.' We weren't really talking for a long time after that." I hadn't thought about that in a long time. Had almost forgotten. "I don't think anyone knew about that, exactly. But Brody got into it with me one night."

"Got into it?"

"With his fists."

"Oh." Elle didn't sound all that surprised. But then again, she'd been there when Brody hit me, back in February; when he accused me of raping Jessa, in front of the whole band. "You mean... that mysterious fractured eye socket and chipped tooth of yours?"

"Right," I said.

That was almost nine years ago now, but I remembered it. Brody had confronted me, asked me if I was sleeping with Jessa. And I'd been just delusional enough at the time to think maybe I could still win her over, that the two of them might give up on each other. Brody had been dating someone else anyway, on and off. I'd managed to convince myself, for a while, that maybe he was just gonna let me have her.

That, and I was probably incredibly high to think that would ever happen.

"And what happened after that?" Elle pressed.

"I kept my distance from her for a while. But after *Love Struck* came out, I tried to get back together with her. The night of her high school grad thing, I showed up outside, wanted to drive her back to Brody's for the party he was having. She said she wouldn't go with me because I was wasted. That was the first time I remember her really having it out with me. She pretty much begged me to get clean, but I was nowhere near doing that. I couldn't even understand what she was going on about. We argued about it. She slapped my face. I don't even know what I said to push her to do that. But I tried to grab onto her when she walked away from me. I caught her shirt and the strap ripped. She cried. It was... awful."

That moment between us was, actually, the worst moment I could remember, because it was the moment when it really got through to me—that I was bad for Jessa. That she deserved so much better than me. That I was just gonna drag her down.

She was beautiful and talented and kind, and she'd just graduated high school. She was barely eighteen. And there I was, twenty-one, trying to drive her to a party while I was fucked up on a cocktail of drugs and booze, trying to talk her into coming back to me, when all she wanted me to do was get my shit together and, probably, leave her the fuck alone.

It was a low, low moment.

But those days, I had a lot of low moments. Most of the time I just tried to annihilate them with drugs.

Got a problem? No worries. Just drink and snort it away.

That night, though, I didn't get any more fucked up than I already was. The argument with Jessa had kind of shocked me sober, or at least sober enough to put her in cab so she could get to Brody's party intact. It was the only time I'd ever come close to putting my hands on her during an argument. She'd hit me first, but that shouldn't have mattered. Loving her and wanting to hurt her; those shouldn't have gone along together. I knew that much.

"That must've been... painful," Elle said, and there was some sympathy in her voice as she studied me. I wasn't sure I deserved it, but there it was. "God knows there was a lot of... well, *drama* in my relationships back then. Still is, sometimes. And Jessa... We all knew she was struggling. She raised a lot of hell for Jesse back then. For Jude and Brody... all of us. I probably would've too, though, if I was in her shoes. Losing her parents so young. Being raised in the middle of this rock 'n' roll circus..." She trailed off.

I had no idea if she meant every word of it, or if she was just trying to encourage me to open up, tell her more about my relationship with Jessa. Baiting me, maybe. Wanting me to feel safe to talk to her, confess my sins, as she measured my responses. I could see it in her eyes. Like a little scale tipping back and forth, weighing the validity of my words. My sincerity.

But on this, I was nothing but sincere.

I had no reason to lie about what went down between Jessa and me.

The damage had already been done.

And it was never me who wanted our relationship kept a secret. It was Jessa who insisted on that.

"Jessa Mayes is a beautiful girl," I said, choosing my words carefully. "But I saw the ugly side of her. That's the worst thing you'll ever hear me say about her, and I don't mean it as an insult. Whatever darkness she had in her, whatever she struggled with, I struggled with worse."

Elle didn't respond, but after a moment she nodded her head, like she wanted me to go on.

"My memories aren't exactly... clear. At least, some of them aren't. Some of them are. Some of them don't even exist. But I *know* I never abused her. Brody accused me of that... of raping her." I shook my head as I spoke. I would never be able to stomach that accusation. "I know I tried to push her in the end, to want to be with me. To love me. To not leave me. But I never pushed her for sex, Elle. I know she was younger than me. But we were both teenagers when we got together."

We were. I was nineteen, she was sixteen, and she instigated sex with me. I remembered, clearly, the first time it happened. We'd taken ecstasy together, and the ecstasy was mine. There was a group of us who'd taken it when we'd gone out clubbing. I didn't intend for me and Jessa to end up alone, in bed, that night. But by then, I liked her. A lot.

I knew how it might sound if I tried to explain that to Elle, so I just said, "I know that doesn't make it right." Because it didn't.

"So what do you think she said? To Brody?" Elle asked me. "To make him think you did that to her?"

"I don't know. I don't know what she said. But I know Brody, and I saw what was between them." I did see. That was a big, big love, probably long before I ever came around. "I think, no matter what she said, it's easier for him to believe I forced myself on her or manipulated her into sleeping with me than to think she actually wanted me, even if it was only for a moment in time, and maybe, for the wrong reasons."

Elle cocked her head, considering that. "What wrong reasons?"

I took a breath and said, "Maybe I gave her something at the time that no one else would."

That much was true enough, though I had no idea if Elle would understand what I meant.

Jessa and I had spent a lot of time together writing songs, at first, and that had been our first bond. And I knew she felt comfortable with me. I didn't judge her or have expectations of her or enforce the same rules on her that her brother and the other guys did.

Over time, though, our relationship was definitely fueled by our mutual drug use.

But I wasn't about to go telling Elle, or anyone else, that Jessa had asked me for drugs. That she'd asked me several times before I smoked up with her the first time. And every other time, she'd asked. Including the time we'd first done ecstasy together. She didn't ask me for ecstasy in particular, but she'd wanted to get high.

It seemed irrelevant. And dirty, somehow, to put it on her like that. It felt too ugly, that I'd given Jessa drugs, no matter that she'd wanted them, no matter what my motivations were.

Maybe Brody would always believe I got Jessa high so I could take her to bed. But he was wrong about that. I knew that. No matter how sketchy my memories, no matter what anyone else accused me of, no matter that I was attracted to Jessa. No matter, even, if Jessa remembered it differently.

Elle was silent. She sipped her coffee and seemed to be considering what I'd said.

Did she think I was a creep? A total fucking asshole?

I really had no clue.

Elle had always been kind of a mystery to me. Something unknown, and far above me. Kind of like the stars in the sky were a mystery to your average man; you might understand the basics of how it all worked, but that didn't mean you could stand there in the light and the beauty of it all and not feel small, awestruck and even unworthy.

All I could really do was wait for her to pass judgment on me. She was gonna make up her mind about me one way or the other. There was little I could do about it now but tell the truth. My truth; the only truth I knew.

"Would you do differently, if you could?" she asked me after a while.

"Hell, yes." I didn't even have to think about that one. "Spent a lot of years angry about it, wishing the past away, wishing I'd never taken that first hit, never tumbled down that rabbit hole."

"I mean, would you do differently with Jessa?"

That, I did have to think about. It wasn't the first time I'd thought about it, either.

"No," I admitted. "Probably not. If I was sober, maybe. But as long as substances were involved... I spiraled around a sinkhole for years with my addiction, and until I quit using, there was nothing I could've done differently."

Elle was silent again. And I wondered how well she understood that. Or didn't.

"What about you?" I asked her. "You ever drift down that rabbit hole?"

"No," she said. "Not entirely. I did a little coke, you know, back in the day." She smiled wryly; made it sound like we were old, that comment. But really, it wasn't so long ago that we were just stupid, naive kids rocking our way to the top of the charts... without a parachute. "I did a little ecstasy. I tried some other pills, some speed. I guess I just dabbled, socially. But after a while, it occurred to me I didn't really enjoy it. Everyone around me seemed to be getting fucked up to escape their lives. I didn't want to escape my life." She shrugged. "My life is pretty damn good."

"Yeah. That's one way to look at it. But some people can't handle their lives, even when they're good, you know?"

"Yeah. I see that," she said. "I guess... I prefer a clear head. Most of the time. I still like pot, sometimes. I like a little booze. I like my sleep. I guess I'm the nun of the group."

I shook my head as the sense of awe I already felt in her presence intensified. "You're strong," I told her, and I meant it. "It takes a lot of strength, and character, to stick to what you like, what works for you, when everyone around you is doing something else. And expecting you to partake."

Elle just shrugged that off. "Did the drugs ever work for you? I mean... did you ever enjoy it?"

"Yeah. Hell, yes." It was true. It was so fucking sad, but it was true. "You always love it right before you hate it. And even when you hate it... there are moments when you truly believe you might come to love it again. Right up until it almost kills you."

I watched the troubled look flicker over her face, and I could only guess that she was remembering, all those years ago, when I'd OD'd. When she saw me after I'd OD'd.

Jude had told me about it afterward; that it had been Elle who'd found me, who'd held me in her arms until the medics came to scrape me off the tour bus floor.

And I wished I could remove the burden of that particular memory from her, but I couldn't.

"Do you think... I mean, honestly," she asked me, "do you think if you hadn't gotten involved with Jessa, you still would've ended up where you did? You know... if you didn't have your heart broken?"

I didn't answer; I wasn't sure how to answer.

Despite the things I'd said to Jessa when she confronted me at that cafe back in February—defensive, bitter things—I wasn't sure Jessa *had* broken my heart.

"That's why you overdosed, right?" Elle said. "That's why you went so far down the rabbit hole."

"It wasn't just Jessa, Elle. It was a lot of things." I shook my head. "It was me. Overdosing... getting kicked out of the band... that was all me. In the end, it had shit all to do with her."

But Elle just cocked her head and stared at me, a small, thoughtful frown on her pretty face, like she wasn't sure that was true. As if it was the first untrue thing I'd said to her tonight, and she was trying to make sense of it.

"You must've loved her," she said softly, her gray eyes on mine. "A lot."

I thought about that, like I had so many times over the years, with a kind of question in my heart that I had never really been able to answer.

I knew I'd held onto that idea for a long, long time. That I'd loved Jessa; that she'd rejected me. It was part of the story I'd told myself, *about* myself, to make it okay to keep hurting myself. To fuel the bitterness and resentment I still felt toward her for abandoning me, toward the band for abandoning me; a bitterness I'd only managed to truly put behind me this year. After they left me *again*— and I decided to put the past to rest.

To let it go.

It was a new day. I was a new man.

But it wasn't that simple, was it?

You could stop using drugs and get clean, but you couldn't just wipe the slate clean and leave it all behind. Not when it had all become a part of you, changed you, shaped the whole new you that you believed you'd become.

All the pain I'd been through would always be a part of me, etched into me, along with all the mistakes, the regrets. If for no other reason than to inform the choices I made going forth. So that, hopefully, I would never make those same mistakes again.

In life... or in love.

"I must have," I said, finally.

But the truth of it, the truth I was most ashamed of, was that I didn't wholly remember.

CHAPTER NINE

Elle

AS I WENT UP to bed after talking with Seth, just before dawn, I felt kinda better, in a way. And yet... worse, somehow.

There was just so much pain in Seth's past—in all of our pasts, when it came to him, and Jessa—that I understood why the guys just wanted it to go away. Why they wanted Seth to just go away.

They believed he'd hurt their girl, their collective little sister, and they couldn't stand for that. They felt betrayed by him. And that betrayal hurt all the more because they'd loved him.

Maybe, deep down, they still loved him.

After sitting with him tonight and talking with him, looking into his eyes and listening to him talk, I knew I still did.

I wandered into my bedroom, the room where I always slept when I stayed here—the largest of the guest bedrooms, overlooking the cliffs and the ocean beyond. I tossed my phone on the bed, more or less dreading actually looking at it, and headed into the en suite bathroom. I took a hot shower, trying to let the tension of the day roll off, and thought through what Seth had told me.

After hearing what he had to say about Jessa, I could understand that Brody or even Jesse wouldn't want to hear it. But I still wasn't sure what to believe myself.

I didn't feel like Seth was lying to me.

But I'd learned, living in and out of the spotlight, existing in two somewhat separate but parallel realities—my rock star life and my *real* life—that there were two sides to every story.

And one side didn't necessarily have to be wrong for the other side to be right.

Take me and Jesse.

We were both in that relationship together. But I was in love. He wasn't.

Our breakup, for me, was heartrending. For him, it was probably more of a relief.

There were definitely two sides to that story, and on the best of days, they didn't gel.

After my shower, I slipped into a robe, dried my hair, and forced myself to check my phone. Predictably, calls had started rolling in from everyone and their dog. By now, they all knew Seth was here with me. Probably Jude, who would've heard about it from Flynn, had told someone—Jesse?—and the news had spread, like it did in the Dirty world—like a fucking virus. And they all wanted to know what the hell was going on.

Jesse included. But I didn't call him back.

Brody had called, three times, but I didn't call him back, either.

What the hell would I say?

Jude himself had checked in, and I texted back to let him know everything was fine. Flynn would be keeping in contact with him, but I knew he'd appreciate hearing back from me personally. The last thing I needed was to sound the alarms with Jude and have him flying out here to raise hell. But I did have one question for him.

Me: Why did you let Seth into the audition?

His response came within a minute.

Jude: Because he asked.

A typical Jude response.
I noticed, though, that he didn't ask me why I'd brought Seth to Hawaii.
He didn't ask me anything at all.
Jude and I weren't exactly close enough that I felt the urge to dig any deeper... or explain myself. Best not to crack open that can of worms over text message. Keeping the members of Dirty safe and secure was Jude's job; a job he'd done, and done well, for a decade. But he was also Jesse's best friend, which meant I wasn't all that comfortable having him all up in my personal business.
For the most part, he respected that.
I turned off the lamp and sat down on the bed in the dark, listening to the soft roar of the ocean through the open windows as the sky began to lighten, totally unable to sleep... and eventually, I decided to return Dylan's call. It was still early in L.A., though not as ungodly early as it was here. He'd probably be asleep anyway...
But he answered on the first ring. "Hey. How are you?"
"I'm fine," I said. "How're you?"
"What's going on? I heard Seth's with you."
I took a breath. "He is."
"Why?"
"Because..." How to answer that, exactly? "I invited him to come to Woo's with me."
"Uh-huh. Why?"
"Because I wanted to talk to him and this is where I was headed. So here we are."
"Elle. Everyone's worried. The guys. Ash... Everyone wants to know what's going on."
"I know. But there's no need to worry, okay?"
"Elle..."
"You can tell them I'm fine."
Dylan was silent a moment. "You think *he's* fine?"
I wasn't even sure how to answer that. "Uh, yeah. I think so. I

mean, he probably knows everyone's gonna be upset that I brought him here—"

"Okay," Dylan said. "But I was talking about Ash."

Oh.

"You think he's okay with this?"

"I didn't ask him to be okay with this, Dylan. I don't need his permission anymore than I need yours."

"You're not seeing me, Elle."

"I'm not seeing him, either."

"Since when?"

I sighed. It wasn't like I'd expected Dylan not to find out about me and Ash. I never told him that we'd hooked up at Jesse's wedding or that we'd been hooking up, casually, ever since. But I also never explicitly asked—or expected—Ash not to tell him. And even if Ash didn't say a word, Dylan was close enough to both of us to figure it out on his own.

"Yes, Ash and I had a thing," I admitted. "But it's over now, and it wasn't a real thing anyway."

Silence again.

Then: "Does he know that?"

I didn't respond to that. Of course Ash knew it was over. It had been dying for a while now.

But did he know it wasn't real?

"I'm gonna go, Dylan. I've got messages coming in." It was true enough; my phone had jingled with incoming texts while I was talking to him. The calls and texts would probably be flooding in all fucking day.

I felt weary just thinking about it.

"You sure you're okay?"

"I'm fine. And I've got Flynn." I felt the need to say it, to allay his worries.

"Okay. Take care of yourself," he said. "Call me for anything."

"I will."

"I'll check in later."

"Great."

I hung up from that conversation feeling even worse than before.

I didn't love anyone in the band worrying about me. Normally, I'd find it annoying, like they were playing big brother and getting nosey, and I hated that shit. But Dylan was different. Dylan didn't worry about much, and he knew me; he knew I took care of myself, he knew I had my shit together, that I had a whole team of people to help me keep my shit together, and he knew I didn't need or want him to worry.

But I could hear it over the line. He was worried about this.

I checked my new messages, grudgingly, and found a couple of texts from Maggie.

Maggie: Call Brody. He's freaking out.

Maggie: Let me know if u want to talk. Off the record.

Shit... If Maggie said Brody was "freaking out," things were not good.

I sent her a quick *Thank you* for the off-the-record offer. Maybe I'd take her up on it in the future. Not right now, though.

Right now, I still hadn't figured out my own take on the whole Seth situation. I wasn't ready to discuss it with anyone else.

Me: How's Jesse?

I sent the question to Maggie, like I had many times this past year when I was concerned about him, or curious, or whatever, but didn't want to speak to him directly.

Maggie: Not sure. Katie says he's been out all night drinking with Jude and before that he was pacing a lot.

Maggie: Whatever that means.

Maggie: It's a shit storm over here.

She punctuated that with a smiling shit emoji.
I cracked a smile.

Me: Sorry for causing the shit storm.

Maggie: Not your fault.

Maggie: Men.

She sent another smiling shit emoji.
Then a call came through. The pop-up on the screen read: *Jesse. Wonderful...*
I took a breath and answered the call. "Hi."
"Hey. How you doing?" He sounded tense. Really tense. Drunk?
"Good."
"You at Woo's?" His voice was clipped, gruff.
"Yes."
"How long?"
"A few days. Maybe a week. Why?"
"Seth there with you?"
"Yes."
Silence.
"What do you want, Jesse? I'm on vacation, okay?"
"With Seth Brothers?"
"As it turns out."
"And how *did* that turn out...?"
"Jesse. I really don't have to explain myself to you."
"Like hell you don't."
"Jesse—"
"You better start explaining to *someone*, 'cause Brody is climbing the fucking walls—"
"And I'm sorry Brody's upset. But this has nothing to do with Dirty."
It didn't. Not right now.

Right now, it had to do with me and Seth Brothers and that was about it.

"Then what the fuck does it have to do with, Elle?"

"Honestly, it's none of your business."

Jesse huffed and said, "You gonna call Brody?"

"Soon."

"Make it sooner."

"Goodbye, Jesse." I didn't wait for him to say goodbye. I hung up.

This was nothing new, exactly.

So Brody was losing his shit. And Jesse was pissed at me. As usual, everyone had a reaction to every fucking thing I did. An expectation of me. A demand.

Everybody wanted something from me, whether they had a right to or not.

But there was one person I hadn't heard from yet. The one person who actually *had* a right to demand to know what was going on here, if anyone did.

So I called Jessa Mayes myself.

No big surprise, Brody picked up. Once the auditions wrapped, he would've been on the first plane home to Vancouver to be with her. Though he sounded remarkably calm when he told me, "The band knows Seth is there with you."

"And let me guess. They're not happy about it."

"I'd say they're confused, Elle."

"We're just talking," I told him. "You don't want to talk to him, and Jesse doesn't want to talk to him, but I do, Brody."

"And you think this is the way to go about that? There are ways to handle this, Elle. Formal channels. You shouldn't even be speaking with Seth Brothers, much less jetting off to Hawaii with him, without a written contract beforehand to protect yourself."

"I don't need a contract to have a conversation with an old friend," I told him.

There was an ugly silence, at the end of which he said, in a low voice, "You need to think about protecting the band, Elle."

"This isn't about the band."

"Then what the hell is it about?"

"Can you please put Jessa on?"

"She's busy."

"Is she there with you? I called to talk to her."

"*Brody!*" I heard Jessa, somewhere in the background, and I could just picture her: standing there with her hands on her hips as Brody held her phone out of reach.

I took a deep breath and forged on, forcing out the words I did not particularly want to say, but had to. "Brody, don't you think that if I'm sitting here with a man who raped Jessa Mayes, that I have a problem with that, and maybe I need to hear it from her if that's *not* the case?"

I heard some fumbling and then Jessa's voice again, muffled. "*Jesus, Brody!*" There was more fumbling, then Jessa was on the line. "He didn't... Is that what Brody told you? That Seth *raped* me?"

"No," I said, relieved to have her on the phone. "Not directly. But that's what he said to Seth when he broke his nose, right in front of the band."

"Oh. My. God. *You broke Seth's nose?*" That was muffled, and clearly aimed at Brody. I heard him grumble a reply, but I couldn't make out the words.

"We, uh, all heard him say it," I told her. "So you can imagine how that's left us all... disturbed."

"Um, yeah. I'd say so." Jessa did not sound happy. Clearly, she had no idea what actually happened that night. Had no idea what Brody had accused Seth of in front of all of us. "Seth Brothers is not a rapist, and he didn't *do* anything to me. So if you hear Brody or my brother say any such thing, you can tell them to—oh, God. *Yuuuck.*"

I sat up, alarm spiking through me. "You okay?"

"*Ugh...* The baby just rolled over. I swear, it's like having an alien inside you."

"Oh." I exhaled. "Sorry to be calling you with this, Jessa, really. I know it's bad timing." It was. Clearly.

"It's fine..." But there was a groan of discomfort in her voice.

"I'll let you go. I didn't mean to upset you. I just really need to know... Are you okay with me talking to Seth? He's here with me, in Hawaii. We're at Woo's place."

"Elle, you don't need my permission. You can talk to whoever you want to." Then she whispered into the phone, "Brody's pissed, though."

"I noticed."

"I'm sorry, I should really go. The baby's all kicky in the morning and Brody's gonna pop a knuckle squeezing his stress ball. I need those hands to massage my hips and my swollen feet or I won't get any sleep. I barely slept all night."

"Of course," I said. "Tell him, for what it's worth... I'm sorry. I know he doesn't want you upset right now."

"I'm not upset, Elle. Just..." Her voice softened. "Be careful, okay? Addicts can be... unpredictable."

"I will."

I didn't know for sure if I could believe her, that she was one hundred percent okay with me talking to Seth. But whatever problem she might've had with it, she clearly wasn't going to try to put it on me.

And at least now I knew, for sure, that the man in the cottage outside wasn't a sex offender. So that was something.

A rather large something.

"Brody says he'll call you later," Jessa said. "Take care, Elle."

"Take care of yourself, and that baby."

When she'd hung up, I flopped back on the bed, relieved.

And yet...

Even though Jessa herself had just adamantly stated, right in front of Brody, that Seth had never abused her like Brody seemed to think he did... I did not see everyone just doing a massive one-eighty and welcoming him back to the band tomorrow with open arms.

I tossed my phone aside and groaned aloud.

What a fucking mess.

I still couldn't blame Brody, though. He was, as usual, trying to protect the band. He was trying to protect me. And of course, he was trying to protect Jessa and their baby.

He'd gotten her pregnant, accidentally, sometime after Jesse's wedding. Basically, as soon as they started sleeping together, as far as I knew. But despite what had happened today, I had never seen Brody happier. Jessa and that baby were everything to him.

She was almost seven months along, and given that she was a slim girl to begin with, she'd gained a lot of baby weight. It was a big stress on her body and she'd confided in me that she was having a lot of joint pain and discomfort. Nothing terribly unusual, according to her doctor, but I'd be disappointed in Brody if he *wasn't* worried about her.

I didn't love adding stress to his plate with all that he was already dealing with, and I knew, no matter how devoted he was to Dirty, his family—Jessa and that baby—would always come first.

But as I shrugged off my robe and slipped in under the covers, and I thought about how this day had ended, I knew it in my heart: I wouldn't change a thing.

There was something compelling me to talk things through with Seth. To try to get to the heart of the matter.

Maybe because I'd never been able to believe, no matter what had gone down between Seth and Jessa, that he could've done any such thing as force himself on her, either physically or by manipulating her.

And if Brody's accusation really was unfounded, as Jessa herself had just told me, then the band had no reason to condemn Seth for preying on Jessa. She was young when they got together—they both were. But could he really be blamed, a nineteen-year-old young man, for screwing around with a sixteen-year-old girl?

Not in my world.

When I was sixteen, I'd dated a twenty-two year old, and none of my friends had bat an eye. Even my parents had been fine with it, once they met him.

All that left, really—if Brody and Jesse could put aside their bloated male egos and forgive Seth for having a relationship with

Jessa at all—was the fact that Seth had done drugs with Jessa behind our backs.

Maybe that was a much more difficult trespass to forgive.

Because in the end, maybe that drug use had driven her away from us.

Away from Brody.

And as I considered that, I knew... Brody would have a hell of a hard time ever forgiving that.

As I lay here, alone, unable to sleep, my thoughts turned to Seth, alone in his cottage. In my thoughts of him over the years, he was always alone. I could never picture him any other way. A lone wolf; that's how I'd always thought of Seth.

But there was something about him tonight... something I'd sensed while we spoke. Something I recognized in myself: a discontent.

Not that he seemed unhappy, exactly. Maybe, now that he was clean, he was content with everything about his life, except for that one essential thing that was missing: Dirty.

I was definitely happy with my life, except for that one thing that was missing.

That incredibly crucial thing.

And I wondered, was Seth lonely, like me?

He didn't *seem* lonely. Not like he had when I first met him... years ago, when he was living more or less on the street and couch-surfing, selling pot, with little more than the guitar on his back. He still had a rare, cool kind of confidence, just like he'd had back then, despite all he'd been through. But now, he seemed more like a man who'd grown into his own skin, who was deeply comfortable with who and what he was.

But nobody would think I was lonely, either.

From the outside, I probably looked like I had the perfect life. Like I had it all figured out and then some.

Yet Seth had straight-up asked me if I was lonely. It was one of the very first things he'd asked me.

I just didn't know why he'd think that.

People were always swarming around me. All day, they were in my space, in my face, even touching me... but yes... at the end of the day, I was alone.

Even when I was messing around with Ash, I went to bed alone.

Sure, if I asked him to, Ash would probably hop on a plane right now to fly out here and put his dick in me. He'd probably even hold me afterward if I wanted him to. But that wasn't the same. It wasn't the same as being *with* someone.

Or being in love...

Because even when Ash was in my bed, in my body—*especially then*—I still felt alone.

CHAPTER TEN

Elle

I EMERGED from my room sometime in the early afternoon, feeling refreshed; I'd finally fallen asleep mid-morning and slept like the dead. The house was empty, but I found Joanie out on the shaded front deck, juggling her laptop and her phone. As of right now, I actually felt like I was on vacation, but technically, she wasn't. Clearing my schedule meant Joanie's was extra full.

I brought a plate of lunch out to her; she said she hadn't had any yet, but Seth had left a salad he'd made in the fridge—topped with grilled chicken breast, local papaya and strawberry guava dressing. Apparently the man was handy in a kitchen.

Who knew.

I took my own lunch out into the back yard, alone, feeling something I hadn't felt much lately: happy to be right where I was.

Joyful, even.

I put on some bright, sunshiny, sexy music. First song up: "Feels" by Calvin Harris, with Pharrell Williams and Katy Perry. Pop and electronic music had become necessary switch-ups for me, to reset and recharge, when rocking my ass off with Dirty had depleted me. Which was why my solo album had been heavily electronic, a mix of electronic rock and straight-up dance tunes. Groove-heavy, bass-driven songs written by me, my girlfriend Summer—who was a fucking killer DJ—and Woo, who'd produced the album.

And I had to admit, ever since Ash had serenaded me with a Calvin Harris song—the night we first hooked up—I'd become hooked on Calvin Harris's music. Not because it reminded me of Ash. Because it reminded me of letting go, of moving forward; of better times to come.

After I ate, I reclined on one of the long lounge chairs on the patio in my bikini, still feeling a little tired. It was my favorite bikini, my sexiest bikini, the one I wore when I wanted to catch some sun *and* feel good about myself. I wouldn't have worn it if Seth or Flynn were here—it was that sexy. But Joanie said Seth had gone shopping, and I knew Flynn would keep himself scarce until he was needed, which meant neither of them would be subjected to my near-nakedness in my custom-made cream crochet bikini. My *unlined* crochet bikini.

Not only was it skimpy, it had holes in it. The breeze went right through it. If you had the balls to look really, really closely, you could see my nipples through it... among other things. I always made sure I was *completely* shaved before putting it on.

Kinda felt like being naked, without actually being naked.

In fact... it felt kinda like a waste that no one was here to see me in it. On further consideration, it was really more of a bikini you wore to catch some sun, feel good about yourself *and* show off for a man.

So I did the next best thing. I took a hot selfie and sent it to my most incredibly-supportive girlfriend, one who always appreciated sexting, even if it only came from me.

Summer: Hawt!!!!!

Me: Kauai baby!

Summer: Hope you brought a man with you.

Summer: Or an anatomically-correct toy.

I hesitated to respond.
But it was Summer; I told her pretty much everything, and God knew she was not shy—at all—about telling me every fucking detail of her intimate life.
So I replied...

Me: I brought Seth.

Summer: Whatnow?

So I guessed she hadn't heard about the big scandal yet.

Me: Don't ask.

Her responses came in, rapid-fire:

Summer: I'm asking

Summer: Considering you're wearing the worlds tiniest excuse for a bikini...

Summer: Maybe I don't need to ask?

Summer: Ok I'm asking

Summer: Seth Brothers, right?

Me: The one and only.

Summer: When did this happen??

Me: Nothing happened.

I considered adding, *We're just friends.* But I didn't know if we *were* friends.

We used to be. And I knew I still wanted to be. Maybe that's what this was all about. Salvaging a friendship, if a working relationship was out of the question?

And in that case... maybe it was up to Seth if we were friends.

Me: We're talking.

Summer: Uh huh. You've been known to wear that to biz meetings.

Me: He's not here.

Me: I'll get dressed before he gets back.

Summer: Or don't.

Then she sent a devil face.

Me: I could wear this to talk to entire band and maybe they'd listen to me for once?

Summer: Mmm... not.

Summer: Sorry, hon. Gotta go. Strutting into lunch meeting.

Me: Your life is so glam

Then I sent her a series of hearts and kissy faces. Because I loved her like that.

Summer: You know it. Check in later babe.

Summer: Where's Ash?

Right. Ash.

Summer's ex-boyfriend.

The two of them were still good friends. Such good friends that she had no problem whatsoever with me hooking up with him, as evidenced by the fact that she'd given me the green light, long before we hooked up, "just in case." Maybe she'd sensed he was into me. Either way, I'd never felt bad hooking up with him, where she was concerned; there was no need.

But somehow, I felt bad about her finding out I was cutting him loose. Because she was still protective of him, even if not possessive.

Me: He stayed back.

Me: Talk later babe. XO

I figured I had a little wiggle room, maybe, to wait to talk to her about it in person. In case she was upset about it.

Obviously, he hadn't said anything to her about it yet.

I lay back and just tried to chill out about it. About everything. Fortunately, it didn't take too long to get there. It *was* Hawaii. Chill was in the air.

Besides that, Bruno Mars was playing, "That's What I Like." While I lay there, actually feeling relaxed for the first time in weeks —if not months—*and* all kinds of sexy, I wondered, briefly, if I'd made a mistake not bringing Ash here with me.

But I knew that was just my horny, almost-naked pussy talking.

The rest of me was glad Ash wasn't here. Especially when he texted me not long after.

Ash: What's the deal with Seth?

I wasn't sure if he was asking what was going on with Seth and Dirty, and/or with Seth and *me*, but if he was being passive-aggressive and accusing me of something—messing around with Seth?—

while trying to pass it off as concern about the band, it was thinly-veiled.

At that point, I turned off my phone.

And I thought about what Joanie had told me.

She said Seth had gone to buy some clothes, since he hadn't brought any extra with him. She'd told him Woo had some random stuff in the guest rooms he could use, but he declined that. Maybe he didn't want to impose. Maybe he felt uncomfortable here, but apparently he'd been nothing short of completely courteous with Joanie and Flynn. He'd gone grocery shopping with Joanie this morning and made everyone fresh-squeezed orange juice and banana pancakes, which I didn't even know was a thing, despite the Jack Johnson song.

Joanie had even caught him chatting with Flynn over coffee, out in the driveway after breakfast, and it was rare that either of us caught anyone chatting with Flynn. The man didn't exactly talk much. But apparently, he and Seth were now coffee buddies.

Never saw that coming.

I had to wonder if Seth had even slept.

I knew he'd been careful with me, feeling me out. Letting me work on the plane. Not pushing for conversation. Clearly, he was letting me take the lead in how things unfolded between us. I knew this was on purpose and I not only appreciated it, I respected it.

Too many people in my life did not know when to back off and give me space. Or, frankly, shut their mouths.

As the afternoon waned, I felt closer to being ready to talk to him some more. To *really* talk. And maybe let my guard down a bit. The sleep and the sunshine had helped me to process what we'd discussed last night. By now, I'd pretty much cooled off. Any anger I'd felt at the audition, and afterward, had dissipated. It was really just a knee-jerk reaction, based on things that were long in the past.

And anyway, I'd had an epiphany today.

Last night, after we'd talked, Seth had asked me if I thought I could ever forgive him. I couldn't really give him an answer, but not because I couldn't forgive him. It had only started to become clear to me when I woke up this afternoon: I didn't really believe in forgiveness.

For a long time, after Jesse broke up with me, I wanted him to forgive me. I kept waiting for him to change his mind and ask me to get back together with him, and when that didn't happen, I started hoping he'd forgive me for whatever I did that was so wrong. I even asked him, once, if he was ever going to do that.

He'd looked completely stunned by the question.

Because of course, there was nothing to forgive. It wasn't like he was mad at me for what happened between us, for our relationship not working out. At first, I was kind of confused about that. How could I make amends with him if there was nothing to forgive? Maybe I magically wanted something to change, to make things better between us.

But that wasn't going to happen overnight.

We'd shared an intimacy that, in the end, hadn't worked for us, and now we had to live with it.

His way of living with it was to move on—big time.

For me, it had taken a lot longer.

But as time passed, I'd come to the realization that I actually hadn't done anything wrong in that relationship. I was just me, and that wasn't what he wanted.

I didn't need anyone to forgive me for that.

And I didn't need to forgive Seth Brothers for being who he was. No matter how much his actions had hurt me, hurt the band, hurt himself, he didn't need forgiveness from me. In my mind, forgiveness implied that you were better than someone else, that they were seeking some kind of absolution from you. And that felt all wrong to me. I didn't want to have that kind of power over anyone.

I wasn't better than Seth, just like Jesse wasn't better than me. So I wasn't looking to forgive or to be forgiven anymore. We'd all made mistakes. We were all entitled to carry on, to make mistakes again, to do our best. To be human.

Personally, all I really wanted was to be free to be *me* with the people who were closest to me—flaws, fuck-ups and all. Not Elle the rock star. Just Elle.

And to be loved for who I really was.

That meant accepting other people as they really were, too.

Like Jesse. Because Jesse Mayes was not the man of my dreams; I'd come to accept that much. He was just Jesse.

And now, he was Katie's husband.

The man of *her* dreams.

I wanted to look at him without seeing all the mistakes we'd both made, and just see *him*—without wanting things to be any different than they were.

And ultimately, that was the same thing I wanted with Seth.

I just wasn't sure how to explain all of that to Seth without sounding cheesy or insincere—given how I'd essentially dropped the ball on our friendship for so damn long—or rambling on about The Great Lessons I'd Learned From My Broken Heart... Or how to show him.

Maybe bringing him here was a first step?

Maybe that's why I knew it was the right thing to do, even if everyone else disagreed.

I just knew I had to find out who the man really was. Because how could I get to making peace with the past, accepting Seth as he was—then and now—and being any kind of friend to him, when I didn't even know that much?

As of right now, I was willing to start fresh. To wipe the slate clean of assumptions and give him a chance.

The fact was, it had been years since Seth and I had spent time alone together. And we'd never spent time together when he wasn't using, until this year. For all I knew, back then, I'd never had a conversation with Seth Brothers when he wasn't under the influence of drugs.

How could I possibly make a decision on where he fit with the band, or where he fit into my life, if we didn't even know each other anymore?

And maybe, to be fair to both of us, we never really did.

"Mai tai?"

Sometime later, I looked up to find Seth strolling across the patio toward me, a cocktail in hand. It was colorful and drool-worthy, with a chunk of pineapple on top and a little umbrella.

I sat up a bit. *Shit...* I'd fallen asleep.

"Thought you could use a cabana boy," he said. "You know, get the full tropical vacation experience." He stopped right next to my lounge chair, which I'd dragged into the shade of one of the giant umbrellas when the sun got too high and hot.

"Thanks." I smiled, tentatively. "I've always wanted my very own cabana boy." I stretched a little and reached to take the drink. As I did, Seth's gaze flickered down my body.

And I remembered what I was wearing.

My X-rated bikini.

I took the mai tai and sank back into my chair, a little embarrassed. My playlist was still rolling, Maroon 5's "Sugar" playing, and I felt awkwardly like the star of my own sexy swimsuit video. I could hardly blame him for looking; even Dylan checked me out when he once saw me in this thing, and Dylan was the closest thing to a brother I'd ever had.

As much as Seth and I had once been bandmates, tourmates and friends, he had never felt like a brother to me.

This was evidenced by my own gaze, dropping south of his face. He wasn't wearing a shirt. I'd actually rarely seen Seth without a shirt. Unlike Jesse, who rarely ever wore a shirt onstage, Seth pretty much always did. And come to think of it, he'd never been one to lounge around half-naked like the other guys seemed perfectly comfortable doing. Not because he was uncomfortable with it, but because he'd never been the attention-whore the other guys were.

Which, in a way, was kind of a shame. For the female fans.

His shopping trip must've been successful because his jeans were gone, and in their place, thin white cotton pants sat low on his hips.

He was slimmer than Jesse and Ash. I wasn't sure why I made that comparison in my head, but there it was.

He was tight though, toned, and cut in all the right places. My gaze followed the suggestive V of his groin down, where it disappeared into his pants... then shot up again, quickly... over his tight abs and his hard chest, to his face. His olive-toned skin set off his grayish-green eyes... which seemed to darken as he looked down at me.

"I wasn't gonna offer to rub lotion on you or anything," he said slowly. "That's where I draw the line."

"Uh... that's okay," I said. "Joanie already took care of that." Then I laughed a little, thinking I was being funny. Though I realized, belatedly, that now he was probably just picturing Joanie rubbing lotion on me, which was not what I'd intended. Joanie was cute, with her strawberry-blonde hair and rampant freckles. And in this bikini, I was obscene.

That mental image was total spank bank material.

I cleared my throat a little. I'd just woken up; maybe that's why everything felt a little off. That, and the fact that I was practically naked. In front of Seth.

"Cheers," I said, raising my drink. It was cold, the glass already dripping with condensation, and I was definitely in the mood for a cold one.

He raised his coffee mug—which I really hoped *was* just coffee —and we clinked. "Cheers."

I took a sip of the mai tai. It was delicious, but I hoped he hadn't taste-tested it. Who knew what a simple sip of fruity cocktail could do to a reformed heroin addict? Not me.

I managed to squeeze out, "Uh... catch up with you later?" as I grew ever more self-conscious in my barely-there bikini.

"Later," he agreed. His gaze flickered over my bikini again—or my body *in* the bikini. Then his eyes met mine. His face was carefully blank, and I had no idea what he was thinking.

Well... I had some idea.

He slid his shades, which had been sitting on top of his head, over his eyes.

Then I watched him walk away, across the patio and the lawn, out toward the trees and the rocky path that led down to the beach. His back was as impressive as his front, which was saying a lot. Seth's face was incredibly easy on a girl's eyes. He had those soulful, smoky eyes and full, kinda pouty Brad Pitt lips. His toned, tanned back and his tight butt in those low white pants were much the same—drool-worthy.

Objectively speaking... Seth Brothers was totally hot. The fangirls had always loved him, and anyone could see why.

But in my estimation, he was hotter now than when he was with Dirty. He'd been younger then, still boyish, and a junkie. Out of control and reckless, and the girls had liked that about him, too.

Now he was a man, though, which meant he had more to offer. To the fans. To any band that got involved with him.

To any woman who got involved with him.

And what fangirl wouldn't like that?

Yeah. If we could only find a guitarist as talented as Seth, who could also sing like Seth, write like Seth, and look like Seth...

I settled back in my seat with a sigh and took a cooling sip of my cocktail.

If only Seth Brothers had an identical-looking, identically-talented twin brother who *hadn't* broken our hearts... we'd have it made.

CHAPTER ELEVEN

Elle

AFTER DINNER, I found Seth sitting on the back patio, alone. Joanie had found us a luau to go to, but I really just wanted to stay in, so we'd grilled some fish instead. Or rather, Seth had grilled some fish. He wouldn't even let me toss the salad to go with it.

I still wasn't sure if the man had slept.

He was seated in front of the stone fire pit where several chairs were arranged, facing the ocean. As I walked up, he was strumming out a song on an acoustic guitar that wasn't his. Several other acoustics were propped up on the chairs, or lying in open cases that had been carefully laid out on a blanket in front of him. He wasn't singing, but as I grew closer, I recognized Paul McCartney's "Band On the Run."

And I stood listening for a while.

Seth was one of those natural guitar players who learned songs quickly and made what he did look easy, even when it wasn't. I knew he would play for the rest of his life, even if Dirty never took him back, even if he never made another penny from playing. He could play with his eyes closed, could probably play in his sleep, and when he wasn't playing, he was writing or humming or tapping out a rhythm with his fingers. The music was just in his blood.

I'd known a lot of musicians like that. Musicians who were crazy-passionate about music, who oozed talent and seemed to eat, live and breathe what they did. Like Jesse and Dylan. But I knew very few musicians who actually gave the impression they might die without music in their lives.

Zane was like that.

And Seth.

And both of them were addicts, so go figure... maybe there was some connection there.

They were also both incredibly cool, but Zane had a jagged edge that, as a woman, I'd never wanted to get near. Seth had an edge of his own, but it was far less... volatile. And he was always kind of a mystery man. He never seemed to crave the admiration of the fans the way Zane did, yet he had this effortless charisma that was magnetic, made people want to be around him. The guys liked Seth. The girls liked Seth.

Just like the other guys in Dirty, he was a man born to be a rock star.

As he reached the end of the song, he started into a classic Dirty tune, "Runaround."

Then he seemed to sense me standing here and faltered; he glanced over, at my sun dress flickering around my bare thighs in the breeze. His hands went still on the guitar and his eyes met mine.

"Woo said I could help myself to the guitars in his studio," he said, like he felt the need to explain. Then he removed the guitar from the chair beside him, clearing a space for me.

"He must hold you in high esteem," I told him. "Those are his babies." I sat down in the empty chair, facing the fire. "You spoke to Woo?"

"This morning. Thought I should, since I'm here."

I wondered what else Woo had said to him, but I didn't ask. "Have you slept at all?"

"Not yet," he said. Then he added, "Didn't really feel like I could."

"Why?"

His eyes left mine. "Hard to sleep, thinking you might hate me."

My stomach turned. My chest squeezed as I said, "I don't hate you, Seth. You can sleep if you want to."

He nodded, but didn't look at me. And my heart ached. My throat constricted with emotion, with sympathy for him.

I cleared my throat and offered, "You know... I know 'Dirty Like Me' gets all the girls tied in knots, but 'Runaround' was the best song you ever wrote. If you ask me."

"I wrote it with Jessa."

"Yeah. You two were quite the creative team." That was putting it mildly.

I had no idea if he knew that Jessa was back with us, writing songs with us again. Or how he might feel about that if he knew.

My gaze dropped to the mug, half-full on the small table next to him. He'd been drinking coffee again. When I looked up, our eyes met.

"I'm sorry," I said. "I don't know why I keep doing that."

"Doing what?"

"Inspecting what you're drinking. It's like I keep checking to make sure there's no beer can or crack pipe next to you." I was embarrassed to admit it, but there it was.

"Well..." he said, processing that, "caffeine's my only real vice these days. And crack was never my thing. Sorry to disappoint." Then he smiled a little, the dimple flickering in and out of his left cheek.

It was the first time I'd seen that dimple since we'd played together in Vancouver earlier this year. I'd almost forgotten he had one.

"I'm sorry, Seth," I repeated. And maybe I was apologizing for a whole lot more than just scrutinizing his coffee.

"Don't be."

I watched as he lay the guitar he'd been playing back in its case.

He was wearing the BADASS cuff bracelet I gave him when he joined Dirty ten years ago. He was always wearing it, every time I saw him, and in every photo I'd ever seen of him over the years. It was pewter, a little worn now; I would've thought he'd replace it with something... well, more expensive.

But he never did.

"It was a lot of fun," I told him, "playing with you again, at the show in Vancouver."

"Yeah. The big reunion." He settled back in his chair. He was wearing linen pants now, rolled up below the knee, and a pale-green T-shirt with the logo of a local restaurant on it; in the early-evening light it made his smoky eyes look more green than usual as he studied me. "I was glad you all let me do it."

"Me too," I admitted. "You fit right in, just like you always did."

He did. Right from that very first day Zane brought him home to jam with us at nineteen. So quiet, kinda shy... until he strapped on his guitar and plugged in and played "Free Bird"—and we all flipped our shit over him.

All the way to that last night... the final show of the first world tour, after which we'd fired him because he was such a fucking mess.

A mere month after he'd OD'd on the tour bus.

He'd come back from the hospital strong, telling us everything was fine, that he was off the heroin. Lying to us, the way addicts did. But we all knew he was sliding down a very deep, dark hole, and none of us knew how to save him from it. We were young enough, maybe, to think we could, for a while.

But then that night, after the last show, he'd gotten high again. Disastrously high. And the rest... was history.

"You were clean at the Vancouver show," I said bluntly, because he was. I could see it in his eyes. "You're clean now."

"Yeah," he said.

"How long have you been clean?"

"Four years. And four and a half months, give or take a day or two. I used to track the days. Now I just do the months." He was looking at me, squinting a bit in the setting sun. "But you know that.

We went over it when you guys hired me back. I told you everything then."

He did. He'd sat down with the band and Brody and told us exactly that. Still...

"I'm asking you now," I said.

And so he told me.

For an hour or so I just sat and listened while the sun went down and the stars started to come out, and he told me everything. What happened after he was dismissed from the band. The almost three years of bouncing in and out of rehab, trying to get clean, trying not to get clean, and the last time, when he actually did get clean—and stayed that way.

I wanted to know about all of it. I wanted to know what it took to overcome that kind of addiction. And when I asked him, he simply said, "Underneath it all, my motivations had to change."

"What were your motivations for using?"

He seemed to consider that for a moment, searching for the right words. Then he said, "I had some demons to battle. Getting fucked up was one way to avoid that battle."

"What kind of demons?" I asked, though I had some idea.

Demons from his life as an orphan. As a foster kid. As a street kid. Demons from his rapid-fire launch into fame. And demons, maybe, that looked like Jessa Mayes.

But he just said, "All kinds."

So I left it at that.

Instead, I asked him about what he'd been doing, musically. I had some idea about that, too, but not much.

He told me about the various other bands he'd played with, none of them lasting. Right up until the day when he ran into Zane on the beach in L.A., and Zane asked him to jam... which led to reuniting with Dirty this year.

"He was excited about reconnecting with you," I told him, remembering the call I'd gotten from Zane. "I think he was relieved, thrilled to see with his own eyes what we'd all heard about you, but been afraid to trust. That you were clean. That you were doing well."

Seth's gaze held mine in the firelight. "And how did you feel about that?"

And I told him, honestly, "Happy. Actually, it was the first time I felt truly happy this year." I pulled my legs up into my chair, hugging my knees, remembering that feeling. "January twenty-second. That was a good day."

"That was just after Jesse's wedding," he noted.

"Yeah."

He was studying me, and I felt the male appreciation in his gaze as it skimmed over my legs. It wasn't a forward thing. More of an involuntary thing, like he couldn't help noticing my bare skin.

And I wondered, had Seth ever looked at me like that, in the past? And if so, why hadn't I noticed?

"What was it like watching him marry someone else?" he asked me.

I cringed a little, because it still wasn't my favorite subject.

"What was it like getting kicked out of Dirty," I asked him, "and watching us play your songs without you?"

"Honestly?"

"Yes."

"It was heartbreaking," he said.

Yeah. Even as I felt the blow of his words, I knew that much.

Because that's how it would've felt for me, if I was in his place.

"It must've been terrifying," I ventured, because that's also how I would've felt. "I mean... you had us. You had management, lawyers and accountants, security, a crew, and then..."

"And then, overnight," he finished for me, "I had nothing. Nobody would talk to me."

That part, I couldn't even imagine. I didn't want to.

It still flooded me with guilt.

"I felt alone, for a long time," he said. "Abandoned. I had no idea what I was gonna do. Dirty was everything to me. The band was the only place I'd ever felt like I belonged. It felt like I'd lost everything."

"I can't imagine," was all I could say. I still felt deep, deep regret over the whole thing, but I knew he wasn't telling me these things to make me feel bad. He was just being honest, which was what I'd asked him to do. "But I'm glad you kept playing with other bands."

"Yeah. I kept playing," he said. "But none of them could replace what I had with Dirty. So I never stuck around for long. I always found some excuse to leave, or to make them ask me to leave. I think I was holding out for Dirty, even if I didn't want to admit to myself that's what I was doing."

"You still wanted to play with us? All that time?" That surprised me, actually. "After we'd fired you?"

"Shit, yeah," he said. "For years I wanted to do some kind of reunion with you guys. I became kinda obsessed with it. I tried reaching out to Brody, to Zane, to all of you. I just wanted to have my moment, you know? To play with you again, even just once, to prove to all of you, to the fans, and to myself, maybe, that I wasn't just some pathetic junkie. I wasn't a fuck-up. I hadn't destroyed the best thing I had going in my life, to the point of no return. That I could still be a part of it again. But no one would have that conversation with me. Zane was the only one who talked to me at all, and he wouldn't go there. So at some point, a few years back, I stopped asking. I figured you guys would come back to me, when you were ready. When the time was right." He shook his head. "I convinced myself that had to be the reason why you never really replaced me. Because you were still holding the spot for me."

"Maybe we were."

He didn't say anything to that, just stared at me. I wasn't sure if I'd shocked him or what. Maybe I'd kinda shocked myself.

But it was true enough.

We'd never said so, never talked about it like that, but there was definitely a hole left behind by Seth that none of us had truly attempted to fill until this year.

"What about Jude?" I asked. "Did you talk to him? Over the years?"

"Sometimes," he said. And I got the feeling that was all I was gonna get. Seth wasn't the kind of person who'd want Jude catching shit for talking to him, and I knew that. So I let it lie. Even though I was incredibly curious.

If Jesse wasn't even talking to Seth, why was Jude?

"And how was the reunion in Vancouver, for you?" I asked him instead. "Was it everything you hoped it would be?"

"Sure," he said. "In a way. But it was pretty bittersweet. I got to work with all these amazing people again. Not just the band, but some of the crew I knew from the old days. And Brody. Got to meet Maggie. Met Jesse's wife." He paused there, like he was waiting for me to say something about that, but I didn't. "But I only got to play the one song. And I'm not gonna lie, that was hard for me."

"Yeah. I guess it would be..." It hadn't really occurred to me, until he'd said it, how hard that would be.

Standing in that bar, watching the show. Watching Ash play his songs, standing in his place.

"It stung. But I just tried to be graceful about it. Be grateful for the moment. Being invited up on that stage at all... Having your trust again, even in some small way."

"It wasn't small," I told him. "We don't invite just anyone onstage with us, Seth."

"Yeah. That's what I kept telling myself. And it did give me some closure, in a way. Just like I'd told myself it would. I told myself I could move on now. Let the past go. Leave all my bitterness and that haunting feeling, that things were still left undone, behind. Stop fantasizing about playing with Dirty again. I could play with other bands and really commit myself to it the way I never had, because I'd been holding out for Dirty. I was finally free to move on."

He looked away. Far away; out over the dark of the ocean.

"And then you did ask me back," he went on, his voice low and thick with emotion. "And it turned my world upside-down. Everything changed overnight. I thought I had it all back." He looked over at me. "Then it got ripped out from under me again. I got dismissed, all over again."

I cringed; I couldn't help it. It was so awful. The entire thing. Losing him again. And Brody's allegations...

"You must've been pissed," I said quietly.

"Yeah, I fucking was. But mostly at myself. I still loved you guys." His voice broke a bit when he said, "I always loved you."

I did not know what to say to that. *We loved you, too* seemed pathetic, given what we'd done to him.

What we'd taken away from him.

He cleared his throat. "These last six months, I played with some other guys," he said. "Mostly because I had to. I had to keep playing for my own peace of mind. But it wasn't right. It wasn't Dirty. The whole time, I think I was really preparing myself to come back, somehow. I thought I was done, but I wasn't fucking done. When I saw the call for auditions, something just snapped in my head. I knew it was my time. It had to be. This was my shot. And once I got that into my head, I wasn't letting it go for anything. Jessa was wrong about me. Brody was wrong. The whole band was wrong. You were all wrong about me, and I was gonna prove it. To you guys. To the world." He shook his head, sighing. "I really, totally believed that. I believed it when I convinced Jude and Liv and Maggie to give me that shot. I believed it when I stepped out onstage, and when I played..."

"I know you did," I said. "I could hear it."

His eyes held mine, just like they did when he'd stood up on that stage.

"But then I saw the looks on your faces," he said. "When you saw it was me. Jesse. Brody. They didn't *want* it to be me. They were so fucking disappointed that it was me. And it broke my heart all over again."

"Seth. I'm so sorry about that..."

"That was the moment I was done. I think the first time I got kicked out of the band, I was too messed up to fully process the loss. And the second time, I was overwhelmed, kinda blindsided by the whole thing. But I wasn't *done*. When Brody told security to kick me out on my ass after I played my heart out for you at that audition...

and I saw you looking at me, so shocked and confused and, I don't know... betrayed... I was done."

The finality in his words sank into me, filling me with a heavy, dreadful sadness. Just like at the auditions, I did not like seeing him give up the fight.

But I also didn't like seeing him fight... and lose the battle.

I hated the way things had gone down at that audition, the way he'd been treated. But I couldn't force the other guys to change their minds about him.

"What will you do now?" I asked him gently. I didn't want him to think I pitied him. I didn't. I respected him, immensely. "Where will you go after this?"

He shook his head and gave up another heavy sigh. "I don't know. Maybe go up to Vancouver, visit Ray. Lay low for a while. He was pretty happy when I told him I was coming up for the auditions. Pretty disappointed when I changed my mind and auditioned in L.A. instead."

"I didn't know you did that."

"I wanted to be last," he said, shaking his head again, like he couldn't believe his own foolishness, "so you wouldn't forget me."

"We've never forgotten you," I told him.

A silence fell, filled only with the soft roar of the ocean and the crackle of the fire. Seth's eyes held mine, shining a little in the firelight, and he nodded slightly, as if to say *Thank you for that.*

I swallowed, trying to loosen the knot in my throat. I hugged my knees tighter against me, though it wasn't cold. "I've popped in to see Ray a few times over the years," I offered, looking to change the subject a little.

"I know," he said. "He told me. You never returned my calls, though. I would've thanked you for looking in on him. I remember you did that, back then, too. Even when I couldn't."

"I always liked Ray."

"He likes you, too."

I knew that was true. And maybe, part of the reason I'd felt it was important to look in on Seth's foster father whenever I could was because Seth would've liked that. I always knew if Seth wasn't so messed up himself, he'd be looking in on Ray more.

"I'm sorry I never took your calls, Seth. I guess... I just wasn't ready," I told him honestly, "to move on from the way you'd hurt us. It still felt too fresh, even years afterward."

"I never meant to hurt you guys."

"I know," I said. "But you did."

He was silent for a moment. Then: "I'm sure there was no love lost for Brody."

"Don't say that. Brody always liked you. It's just... you know how he is about Jessa."

He didn't say anything, just nodded and looked out over the ocean.

"Anyway, I'm not talking about Brody. Or Jessa. I'm talking about the band." But the words didn't feel quite right, and I amended: "No, actually, I'm not. I'm talking about Zane, and me. Losing you was... brutal... for the two of us."

Our eyes locked again, and in that look, I could see Seth's regrets. How much he'd suffered over hurting us. I knew in my heart he never wanted to do that.

His drug abuse was never about us. Overdosing was never about us.

He was headed down that road long before he met us.

And Zane went down a somewhat-similar road himself, before he got sober. We had a lot of growing to do, personally, and as a band. We were such kids when we started out.

We'd all come a long way.

I could already see how far Seth had come. Not just getting clean, but finding some kind of peace within himself that wasn't there before. I could feel it, just sitting here next to him.

And I decided to trust that feeling. Let down my guard a little more.

"You want to play together? Just once?" I shrugged, striving to sound casual about it, when actually, I was itching to play. "You know... for old time's sake."

Seth tipped his chin at the array of guitars before us. "Pull up a guitar," he said, a spark of challenge in his eyes, and I knew he was itching, too.

I took him up on that challenge, pulling the nearest acoustic into my lap.

He selected one, and started right into a song... "Angel" by Jimi Hendrix. Maybe because he knew that I loved me some Jimi.

Maybe because of what that old homeless man said?

Sometimes the angels come a-callin'. Be a fool of a man to pass 'em up...

I followed his lead as best I could. I knew the song, but I wasn't exactly a Seth Brothers-level guitarist, much less a Jimi Hendrix-level guitarist. I was a bassist, but I could hold my own on a six-string. Seth sung as well as I did, arguably better, and I found myself holding back so I could listen to his voice... realizing, in doing so, how much I'd missed it.

Listening to him sing.

Listening to him play.

Just watching him, *feeling* him make music.

Beyond that... there had always been an undeniable chemistry between the members of Dirty when we played together. It's why I knew, no matter what other projects called to me, I could never, ever leave the band. Not only because I loved the guys personally, but because of that chemistry we had, musically. I would've gone so far as to agree that it went beyond chemistry, to something that Zane liked to call *motherfucking magic*.

As Seth and I played by the fire, under the stars, that magic was still here, alive and crackling between the two of us. One song just flowed into another, and another...

And I had so much fucking *fun*.

We played the Rolling Stones, "It's Only Rock 'n Roll (But I Like It)."

We played April Wine, "Bad Side of the Moon."

We played Journey's high-energy anthem, "Any Way You Want It," which Seth sung in its entirety because, of the two of us, only he could pull off anything close to Steve Perry's voice. I joined in at the chorus, and by the end of it we were both smiling, and next, we were laughing.

We played Stealers Wheel, "Stuck in the Middle with You," that cool, classic tune Seth and I used to play together after shows, in the wee hours of the night, in the middle of whatever crazy party we were at, as the two of us avoided the Zane-and-Jesse circus.

We played Trooper, "We're Here for a Good Time (Not a Long Time)," like this really was the last time we would ever play together. Like this was some kind of a goodbye.

The farewell concert.

But all the while, I felt something else catching fire between us, undeniable...

The sparks of a new beginning.

CHAPTER TWELVE

Seth

I FOUND a long rock on the quiet beach, kinda bench-shaped, and sat my ass down on it. It was a small, pale beach in a rocky bay. There was a couple lying on a blanket near the other end, enjoying the sunrise, but otherwise the sand was deserted.

I sipped my coffee, absently, gazing out at the waves. Watching them crash over one another in an endless rhythm.

But in my head, I didn't see the ocean.

I saw Elle in her skimpy bikini.

I hadn't slept much since I got here. Managed to get some sleep last night, but it was full of disturbing dreams. Dreams about Elle. Panicky dreams where I'd lost her. She was there, somewhere, but I couldn't find her. She wouldn't speak to me anymore.

Even with my eyes open, I had Elle on my mind; memories of her, crashing through my head. Memories breaking free from someplace I'd locked up tight and ignored for too damn long. Memories that spending time with her and jamming with her last night had brought back in a flood.

These didn't feel like the kinds of memories, though, that my conscious mind had temporarily lost track of because I'd been wasted—damaged and sketchy and discomfiting. These were pure and bright and oddly painful... more like the kinds of memories that had been consciously suppressed out of some innate sense of self-preservation.

Memories in which I watched a young, effervescent Elle sparkle and shine—from afar.

Even if I was standing right next to her, I held myself at a distance in those memories. It was like watching some movie I knew I'd seen before, and I knew I liked, a lot, though I couldn't recall a single scene until I saw it again, and then it *all* came flooding back to me.

How fucking *lovely* she was.

How much I used to smile when I was around her.

How the whole place—any place—would just light up when she walked in. How the stage caught fire when she was on it, making music, right next to me.

And how I'd told myself—*trained* myself—that I could never get near any of it.

I never even used to stare at her; I was pretty sure of that. Staring at her would've been a bad idea for all involved. I knew that.

But I used to think about her. A lot.

Like I was doing now. Like I'd done every waking minute last night.

I'd definitely forgotten, somehow, how potent it was to be around her. How potent she was. Sexy... all strength and vulnerability. That hot-cold thing that had always intrigued me, secretly confounded me and made me wonder about her... How she could burn like a thousand suns onstage, and then act so damn cool off of it.

And how I'd always been drawn to those two conflicting sides of her—in equal measure.

I'd almost forgotten, even, how I'd let myself fantasize about her... about touching her, just once, to feel that fire ignite between us.

How I'd pictured her, taking off her clothes for me, slowly, baring herself to me, letting down her guard.

Letting herself be vulnerable, with me.

Choosing me.

That fantasy had gotten me so fucking hard the first time I'd really thought it through, suddenly, late one night on the tour bus... it had scared the living shit out of me.

Scared me... but didn't stop me.

I'd jerked off in my bunk thinking about her that night, and for a long while afterward, jerking off thinking about Elle had become a habit. That was just after Dirty had hit the road in support of our debut album, and just like so many of my habits in those days, it was deeply dangerous and self-destructive.

I'd even fucked other girls, back then, thinking about her. Blonde girls. Girls who, if I was just wasted enough, reminded me of Elle.

I'd rationalized to myself that what I was doing was for the best. That it was necessary, even. So I didn't bring any of that misguided lust into my life with the band; with Elle. I'd just screw it out and no one ever had to know.

A man was entitled to his fantasies, right? It didn't mean anything.

And yet, it did.

I could see that now.

I could see how blind I'd been.

It wasn't like I'd totally forgotten about that particular crush... yet I'd managed to convince myself that it was just another fucked-up thing I'd done at a fucked-up time in my life, and swept it under the drug abuse rug.

I'd more or less pretended it didn't happen.

But it did.

And I'd never really examined it.

It was probably the only thing from that time period that I hadn't talked through, in depth, with my sponsor. On my path to sobriety and living chemical-free, I'd talked to him about everything. I'd talked to him about Jessa.

But not about Elle.

Instead, I'd managed to downplay my attraction to her in my own mind. To convince myself it never mattered.

And yet, somehow... it really did.

And now I'd seen her nearly-naked... and I couldn't get it out of my mind. That bikini she was wearing... It was some kind of really loose knit, and through the holes... yeah, I'd seen her. Pretty much all of her. And it seemed to be changing everything. Shifting the Earth beneath my feet in some seismic upheaval, unsettling and resettling my relationship with her so that it felt all weirdly off-kilter.

I knew it wasn't just that I'd seen her like that.

It was that she'd *let* me see her like that.

Maybe she wasn't expecting me to come strolling along while she was on the patio, but when I did, she didn't exactly run away screaming, or even cover up. She looked flushed, a little embarrassed, maybe, but not in a bad way. More like in a self-conscious way, the way you looked when you knew someone was looking at you, but you *wanted* them to look at you.

And then she checked me out. Slowly. Or at least, it felt slow to me. Maybe because it was something I'd wanted so long ago, but believed would never happen, and now that it was happening, I'd only been able to process it that way.

Fucking slowly...

Sitting here on the beach, shirtless, with the warm breeze licking my body... I could practically feel her eyes moving over my bare skin, again. It made my nipples harden. My cock was hardening, just like it started to before I'd walked away... Worse now, because Elle wasn't here to see it, so I didn't try to fight it, to deny it. My balls grew heavy and my cock swelled as I thought about her... her long, lean, tanned body stretched out on that lounge chair beneath me.

Her pussy, pink through the little holes...

Christ. The way she looked up at me... surprised—but not disappointed—to see me. And something else... maybe?

Shit.

Was I this fucked in the head? So fucked up, I couldn't even tell when a woman was sending me signals, and what kind of signals those were?

As much as I'd tried to deny it, ever since Brody accused me of raping Jessa... I had to wonder.

I'd pretty much shied away from getting involved with anyone since then. This whole year, so far, I hadn't touched a woman. Even when I crashed at Lauren's place in L.A.... and her signals weren't so hard to read. I'd known her a long time, and besides, she was vocal about her desires. She'd outright asked me to come to bed with her, but I didn't. When she asked me what the hell was wrong with me, I told her; Lauren was the only one I'd talked to about it, until Elle.

And Lauren's response? She'd laughed.

Then she'd realized I was serious.

How could anyone who knows you think that about you for a second? she'd asked, genuinely bewildered about the whole thing.

At times, I felt bewildered too.

I mean, you're like, the most respectful man I've ever known, Seth, Lauren had said. *I just can't imagine you hurting a girl to save your life.*

I couldn't either.

But tell that to Brody.

"Mind if I join you?"

I looked up at the soft voice, warm tingles shooting down my spine when I realized Elle was there. She was standing on the beach, right behind me.

I sat up straighter, feeling guilty—about thinking with my cock like I'd been doing. I'd totally fucking lost myself to thinking about her. But I looked at her now; all of her. My eyes seemed unable to resist drinking her in, any chance I got.

Might be my only chance.

Any time now, she'd be gone from my life again, and I may never get another opportunity to look at her.

She was wearing a long, loose flower-print dress that fluttered around her in the breeze. She had her arms wrapped around her waist, her hair in a long, loose braid over one shoulder. Little wisps of it were blowing around her face. She looked ethereal and otherworldly, like a mermaid washed up onshore.

Beyond beautiful.

I shifted over on my rock bench to give her room. It gave me the chance to adjust and conceal my rigid dick; luckily I'd worn loose pants.

I swallowed thickly as she came closer, her footsteps silent in the soft sand. My heart was kinda racing and I took a long, shallow breath to try to calm it. She sat down next to me, and I could smell her. Warm and coconuty, sweet and vaguely spicy. Her dress fluttered against my leg. The wisps of her hair tickled my shoulder.

"You look different," she said. She wasn't looking at me, but out over the water. "It took me a while to put my finger on it, but when I saw you without your shirt yesterday... You lost weight since I last saw you." Then her gaze flicked down over my bare chest.

My head scrambled to keep up with what she was saying as I felt her gaze moving over me. "Yeah."

Her gray eyes met mine. "That was barely seven months ago."

It took a moment, but I caught up to that, too. The question behind her words was clear enough: she wanted to know what I'd been doing to lose so much weight, when I really didn't need to lose weight.

Maybe she was having trouble trusting that I was done with the drugs.

If so, I couldn't blame her.

Maybe the entire band had figured there was a pretty good chance I'd spent the last half-year on the receiving end of a needle. Maybe they assumed when they fired me, the second time, I'd just scurried away with my tail between my legs and plummeted straight off the wagon.

But the truth was, I went down south to breathe. To get away from the lawyers and the media and the bullshit. Find my head, get my shit together—and stay clean.

It wasn't easy.

Along the way, I stopped eating, stopped sleeping. I lost twenty pounds overnight.

I also lost some serious respect for myself when I didn't go right back and face down Brody's accusations.

No matter how hard it was, though, I didn't break. If anything was gonna break me, losing Dirty—again—would've done it.

Or seeing that look in Jessa's eyes when she met me in that cafe, after the band asked me back—and she asked me why I didn't just leave.

Didn't you already ruin enough?

Or Brody, putting his fist in my face.

Or Jude, telling me that I was dismissed. Again.

But I didn't break. I didn't once feel the itch—that overwhelming desire to get fucked up.

I didn't think I ever really would again, but I couldn't be sure of that. It would be stupid to believe that. Which was why I still did the meetings, still worked every day at living clean and what that meant to me and *why* I was living clean. Still spoke with my sponsor at least once a week.

But I just told her, "It was a rough seven months."

Elle absorbed that, her eyes moving over my bare chest again, just like they had yesterday. "You do look healthy, though," she concluded. Then her eyes met mine again.

And *damn*... she was gorgeous up close. Like all the rest of her, her face was strong but delicate, with high, Scandinavian-looking cheekbones, though I knew her ancestry was mainly French. Her straight nose with the pretty little tip... her carved lips... all the clean, curving lines of her. And her eyes... cool and gray with little streaks of blue and silver.

I didn't respond. I had no idea what to say. I felt tongue-tied, looking into that face. Seeing the wisdom there, and the control. This was a woman who had her shit together, clearly. I knew it, because when she looked at me, this close, it made me question everything I thought I'd ever figured out about myself.

"I am lonely," she said suddenly. So suddenly it caught me by surprise.

I didn't respond, and she looked out over the water.

"I mean... I have a lot of people in my life," she said. "A lot of friends. Family. But there's a deeper connection that's, I don't know... missing. Some days I ask myself what it is that could possibly be missing from all of this..." She gestured out, over the ocean, gleaming in the morning sun. "And I don't even know. But it *is* missing... and it's not just being in love. I was in love with Jesse, and I still felt alone." Her eyes met mine, and I felt the full force of them, locked on me. "And it's not just feeling wanted. I've been wanted by men and still felt lonely. It's a weird thing, being surrounded by people, being wanted by so many, admired, and still feeling alone. But... I am lonely."

I nodded, like I understood that feeling, and I did, in a way. I'd had a taste of fame. But I was no Elle Delacroix.

"I get that," I told her. "Feeling lonely. But sometimes we feel alone when we're not. I'm sure you've got more love than you could ever know." Because that's what she was saying, right? That's what she was missing?

Love.

"What about you?" she asked. "You've probably still got fans. Legions of them, really."

"I'm not talking about fans," I told her. "I'm talking about people who love who you really are, not who they think you are. *Real* love."

She cocked her head a little. "What happened with your friend with benefits?" she asked, her eyes holding mine, like she was peering into me again, searching for truth. "Melissa?"

"Michelle," I said, though it felt awkward, suddenly, talking about another woman when I was this close to Elle. When I could smell her and see those little flecks in her eyes. When my cock was still half-hard. "I guess... the benefits just kinda faded over time. Friendship felt like a better option, so we went with it."

"That's good. That you're still friends."

I shrugged. "Sometimes it works, afterward. Sometimes it doesn't."

"Yeah," she said softly, and something flickered over her features. Regret, maybe?

Pain?

"How about Ash?" I asked her. "You two still friends?"

Her eyes twitched a little and her face hardened, but I couldn't read the emotion there. "Yeah. Ash and I are friends."

"And what about Jesse?"

"Yes," she said, "we're friends." Her eyebrows pinched together a little and she added, "Of course we're friends."

"Yeah? What happened there? I thought you two were gonna go the distance."

I did think that. Maybe because the media seemed to want the world to think it, and plastered the two of them all over every magazine cover in existence for about a year. Maybe because they just seemed so damned perfect together, like some royal couple of rock. Seemed like what they both deserved—to blaze off into the sunset together.

"Nothing happened." Elle dropped my gaze, looking out at the water again. "I mean... I had this idea about us. He didn't have the same idea. End of story."

But it didn't sound like that was the end.

"And what's it like, playing in the band with him now?"

"It's hard," she admitted. "It feels like..." She sighed. "I think the worst part is that I lost the friendship we used to have. Getting over a broken heart takes time, but it's doable, you know? One day, pretty recently, I think, I just found myself on the other side of it. I'm healing, gradually. And I know I'll be okay again. But we're not the friends we once were, before we got into a relationship. And that's the hardest thing... knowing that Jesse and I can never be friends like that again. Because I just can't trust him the same way I once could. I can't rely on him."

"How do you know that?"

"Because. It's just different now. He has Katie." She looked down, and seemed to be somewhere else for a moment as she watched the water lapping over the sand at our feet. She wiggled her toes, digging them into the sand. "When he's around me, he's not really *here*, you know? It's like he's always on his way to somewhere else. He does everything with her. They're always together. And that changes things. Jesse and I are friends and we'll always be, but..." She shrugged. "He just doesn't have the same room for me anymore. Not like he used to. And maybe that's okay. Maybe that's just how it has to be. I guess... it's all Katie's now."

"And you're okay with that?"

"It doesn't matter," she said, meeting my eyes again. "It's not up to me to be okay with it. I mean... if he was mine... I'd expect her to be okay with it. And if she wasn't..." She sighed again. "I probably wouldn't care about that as much as I'd like to pretend."

"He probably wouldn't expect you to."

She held my gaze a moment as that sank in.

"No," she said softly. "He wouldn't. Which is why I can't blame him for putting her first. Because that's what I'd expect from him, if he was with me."

"Elle," I told her, "you're really strong, you know that?"

She smiled a little, softly, at me. And my chest tightened.

I did not want to lose that smile.

And what about me? I wanted to ask her. *Where do I fit in?* The words were right there, on my tongue, but I didn't ask.

It was a stupid question to ask.

Instead I just watched her as she stood. As the morning sun blazed through her blonde hair.

"Come up to the house?" she asked me, as if she wasn't even sure if I'd come. "Joanie's making breakfast."

"Lead the way."

I got to my feet and followed her up the beach, watching her all the way. Her smooth, golden skin. The low back of her dress revealing the dip in her spine. The way her hips swayed as she navigated the soft sand.

And all the way, I reminded myself that just because she

brought me to Hawaii, and she let me look at her in a skimpy bikini, and she stayed up half the night playing music with me... it didn't mean anything.

Or at least, it didn't mean much.

It definitely didn't mean I should go spinning fantasies of putting my hands on her or ending up in her bed.

Reality was, I *was* gonna have those fantasies now. I knew it as my gaze slid over her heart-shaped ass... I was already having those fantasies. But fantasies were just fantasies.

They didn't have to have any basis whatsoever in reality.

CHAPTER THIRTEEN

Elle

WHEN SETH AND I—AND Flynn, who'd shadowed me to the beach and back—got back to the house, we discovered that we'd picked up a stalker. A photographer with a giant telephoto lens, camped out in the trees just beyond Woo's property line. He'd made himself comfy on the other side of the low stone wall that surrounded the back yard. As if we wouldn't notice him there in the shadows.

Flynn spotted him right away.

"Fucking paparazzi," Joanie muttered, tromping out onto the patio to meet us, where she'd set out our breakfast. Not that the paparazzo was photographing Joanie; Joanie wasn't famous. But I could see how feeling like you were being stalked could ruin your meal, regardless.

"You want me to evict?" Flynn asked me. Clearly, he was chomping at the bit to bounce the photographer out on his ass. Probably bored out of his tree and jonesing for a little excitement.

I didn't exactly enjoy being stalked on my vacation, but I'd learned long ago not to take it personally. Not to let it ruin my meal, much less my day.

"Not yet," I said. Joanie had taken great pains to make crepes, something she'd been working on mastering, and I was determined to enjoy them with my mimosa and the LA Times online. "I'll give him something. Then maybe he'll scurry away."

I had no love for the paparazzi, but I knew how to play the game. It would be best if we just let him get a few shots of us. Doing absolutely nothing. Maybe after we'd finished eating, I'd paint my nails and Seth could trim his beard.

He wanted to invade our personal time? I could waste his like nobody's fucking business.

After that, I'd let Flynn go tell him to fuck off. Flynn could be very persuasive.

But Seth hadn't followed us onto the patio; he'd paused at the gate into the yard, and I turned to watch as he strolled back out toward the tree line—straight on over to the photographer. He had his hands in his pockets, and I watched him chat with the man for a few minutes. Once, he looked back at me.

Then he strolled into the yard and over to me.

"What was that about?" I asked him.

He stood in front of me, shielding me from the photographer with his body.

"I made a deal with him," he said. "Told him we'll give him five minutes to take photos of us on the beach, and then he'll leave us alone for the rest of the time we're here."

"Sounds like a good deal," I said. "For him."

"It's a good deal for all of us," Seth said. "That's Bob Brazer. He pretty much owns this island among the paparazzi. He'll let the others know they can't shoot us either. No one will bother us again."

"You *know* him?"

"Met him a few times over the years. Decent guy."

I snorted in disbelief. I couldn't say I recognized Bob Whatever; I never really looked at their faces. Just saw their camera lenses ogling me, and I usually kept my distance as much as I could. I didn't care to form relationships with them like some celebrities did. To me, they were all cockroaches. Bottom-feeders. At least, the ones who spied on me from the bushes while I was on vacation sure as hell were.

"I doubt that," I said.

"Or I can tell him the deal's off," Seth said, "and we can leave him to Flynn."

I glanced at Flynn. Clearly, he preferred that plan.

"But he might come back," Seth added. "Or someone else might come along. Now that they know we're here..."

"No," I said, glancing from Seth to the photographer. "If you take this guy's word... I'll trust it."

Seth nodded. "Okay."

"*After* I finish my breakfast."

Almost an hour later, I emerged from the house to find Seth and the photographer talking at the edge of the yard. I was glad to see they were standing outside the stone wall; I didn't want that guy on Woo's property. At least he'd changed his camera lens. Since we were actually letting him shoot us, he'd removed the stalker lens and replaced it with a slightly less-intrusive one.

I headed over and Seth met me partway. I'd told Joanie and Flynn to hang back, but let Flynn know he could have words with the photographer if he overstayed his welcome. It was really more of a courtesy mention; Flynn would do exactly that whether I asked him to or not.

Joanie settled in on the patio as we went down to the beach. Flynn stayed back near the rocky path as Seth and I headed out onto the pale, crescent-shaped beach in our bare feet, paparazzo at our heels. I didn't even look at the man; I didn't want to meet him.

Once we reached the water, Seth followed my lead into the rippling surf. There were a few other people on the sand, but they were pretty far away, on the other side of the crescent. We stood in the water facing one another, the waves lapping our ankles. Seth's pants were getting wet. He didn't seem to care. He was wearing those white pants again... and it occurred to me that I was wearing a white dress.

Great choice. Now it probably looked like Seth and I were getting married on the beach.

Technically the dress was off-white, and it was only knee-length, a pretty, flowy, backless sundress. But I wouldn't put it past the paparazzi to print whatever they damn well wanted to.

"Can't wait to see what the caption on this one is," I said, all sarcasm. Mainly because I was nervous. And not exactly about the photos being published. I really didn't care much about that.

A long, long time ago, a very wise man—my dad—told me, *As long as they put my little girl's picture in there and get her name right, it doesn't really matter what they say about her in the article.*

In other words, any publicity is good publicity.

And while I could argue that point, given what I'd been through in the media, at the end of the day my dad was right. People were going to say what they were going to say, publish what they were going to publish, and believe what they were going to believe. There wasn't a hell of a lot, in the end, that I could do about it.

But that never made me nervous anymore. It hadn't in a long time.

Somewhere around Jesse breaking up with me, I'd pretty much given up on caring what the world at large thought about me. That kind of heartbreak had to be recovered from in private, and I'd learned to tune out the voices of the world.

Had to, if I was going to survive it.

But this... *this* made me nervous, for some reason. Standing here with Seth. So close to Seth.

He was looking at me, and that made me more nervous. I could feel it, even though I could only sort of see his eyes through his shades. But he was inches from my face.

I glanced over at the photographer, who was standing on the sand, just out of the water. He'd started taking pictures as we stood here, awkwardly. Together, not together.

At least, I felt awkward.

Seth seemed perfectly at ease.

"Maybe we should just start going at it," he said, and I looked up into his face again. He was smiling a little, the dimple appearing in his cheek. "You know, start making out. They're gonna say it anyway."

I laughed, but it was a weirdly nervous sound, and I hugged myself like I was cold, when I wasn't.

Seth's smile faded, the dimple disappearing. "I'm kidding, Elle."

"I know." He was just trying to lighten the mood, to help me relax. I knew that. But I didn't look him in the eye.

"I'll tell him to leave if you want me to," he said.

"Thank you."

But after the photographer had taken a few more shots, I let my arms drop.

Then I reached out... and took hold of Seth's hands.

He let me.

We acted like we were just hanging out, standing in the surf together, gazing out across the beach. But then I found myself, instead, looking straight down the barrel of that camera lens. Facing it, head-on. Because who the hell were *they*, to judge me?

To judge us?

The media... The band... *Any* of them. They had no right to judge, and I sure as hell didn't owe anyone an explanation for my actions.

Or an explanation for however I felt about Seth Brothers.

The more they demanded one... I was just gonna have to tell them all to go fuck themselves. It was no one's business but mine.

And Seth's.

I held his hands, loosely, as we posed together, sometimes only our fingers hooked together, or our palms sliding over one another's as we shifted position... but we never let go.

And something happened on that beach.

I wouldn't even look at Seth's face. But I could *feel* him. Solid as a rock. His steady, mellow energy, like a kind of healing balm to my nerves, the rolling tide of my defensive anger. I could feel his steady heartbeat in his fingers. The soft strength of his touch and the roughness of his calluses.

I could smell him; his warm, beachy, manly smell... strangely familiar.

And sometimes, when his face was close enough to mine, I could hear him breathing over the soft hiss of the waves lapping at our feet.

I could feel his warm breath on my skin when he leaned into me and said, "You look beautiful."

And I felt the fire rip down my spine.

"I'm gonna go get another round!"

Joanie shouted at me over the music. Despite my hesitancy to leave the peace and quiet of Woo's house, I'd let her drag me out tonight. We were at the Blue Tide, this tiny little open-air bar that we usually visited when we came to Kauai. Me, Joanie, and whoever we'd brought with us. In this case, it was Seth. And of course, Flynn, who chose to hang just outside and smoke under the stars, even though we'd invited him in for a drink with us.

Joanie vanished in the direction of the bar, leaving Seth and I at the table. The place was crowded, as usual. The house band played amazing local music, and the small dance floor was jam-packed. We were sitting alongside the dance floor, Seth in his linen pants and a soft white button-up shirt that was unbuttoned halfway, the sleeves rolled up. His olive-toned skin had darkened the last few days in the sun, and he looked like he belonged here.

That thought warmed me: that Seth had somewhere to belong again.

Even if it was only for a few days.

On the small table between us, he was cupping a coffee mug in his hands as he listened to the band. And I had to admit to myself that the main reason I'd picked this bar over the others on the island was the fact that I knew they served fantastic local coffee at all hours of the night. It seemed unfair to take Seth to a bar and drink in front of him if he couldn't even enjoy a coffee.

He looked over at me, suddenly, like he'd felt me looking at him. Maybe I'd been staring?

I looked away, watching people dance. My legs were crossed and I was swinging one leg to the music, swaying a little in my seat. I only wished I knew the words so I could sing along.

It had been a long, long time since I'd felt this good. This relaxed.

This *carefree*.

Since before my relationship with Jesse, probably. Before things got all tense and fucked up, and daily life became a struggle.

Just get through this day without remembering that you had your heart torn out.

Even when I was screwing around with Ash, and we were having fun... the shadow of that heartbreak was still lurking. I was still running from it.

I wasn't running anymore.

I wasn't sure when it had happened... If it was flying to Kauai, finally getting some time off, or telling Ash he couldn't come with me, or telling everyone else to leave me the fuck alone for a few days... But at some point, it had all stopped haunting me. My broken heart. My struggles to work with Jesse and the rest of the band as if it never happened. My failed attempts to move on.

I finally felt free of it all.

"We should dance." I felt Seth's warm breath on my ear. I turned to look at him; he'd leaned over the table and his face was close to mine. I could see the gold rings around the pupils in his eyes, like fire smoldering through smoke.

And I wanted to dance. With him.

Joanie returned with two ridiculously-girlie pink cocktails in hurricane glasses, setting them down between us. "The waitress will bring more coffee by," she told Seth.

Seth was still looking at me. I nodded at him, and he stood up, extending his hand to me. I swigged some pink drink, then got to my feet, slipping my hand into his.

"We're dancing," I told Joanie. "You wanna come?"

"Nope." She waved us off. "Not drunk enough."

I snickered and shook my head; Joanie was never drunk enough to dance.

I followed Seth as he drew me onto the dance floor. The music was upbeat, mid-tempo. Feel-good music; the easiest music in the world to dance to. And the dance floor was just crowded enough that we had little choice but to dance close to one another.

Really close.

And I couldn't say I minded it. I could feel the heat off Seth's body. His mellow, easy energy. He guided me as we moved, taking the lead. We danced together, but he didn't actually touch me. Other than occasionally brushing into me as the crowd shifted and forced us closer, he didn't touch me at all.

And I was kind of... disappointed.

Because the truth was I kinda wanted to touch *him*.

But if he wasn't gonna put his hands on me, I wasn't gonna make the first move.

Maybe I was just high on the music. Caught up in the dancing. I'd very possibly had a few too many of those giant fruity cocktails with the little umbrellas.

But I wasn't exactly new to this game.

How many times had I been dancing and drinking backstage or at some party or club and had men—hot, *hot* men—rubbing all up on me? That didn't mean I was just gonna lose my shit and spread my legs for every last one of them.

I knew far, far better than that.

I'd always been kinda choosey with men, and I'd learned over the years to become extra choosey. Careful about who I let into my world. And discreet.

Fame had pretty much made that a necessity.

Yet I wasn't exactly being discreet now. I wasn't even sure why.

Why I felt comfortable enough to dance with Seth in public. Sure, it was just some little hole-in-the-wall bar where everyone was dancing and no one seemed to notice or care who or what I was, but I *was* comfortable.

I was more than comfortable.

Comfortable enough to start dirty dancing with Seth Brothers. If he wanted to.

The odd thing about that was, Seth wasn't rubbing up on me. He was very pointedly keeping his hands—and everything else—to himself.

It was so beyond my frame of reference, I almost didn't know what to do with myself. I was used to dancing as a form of foreplay. A pick-up ritual.

Seth was not trying to pick me up.

He was just dancing with me.

I'd always found it incredibly sexy when a man could dance... and Seth Brothers could always dance. I'd kinda forgotten that about him. Maybe I'd forgotten a lot of things, in the end.

Maybe I'd wanted to forget, so I wouldn't have to feel so guilty.

But as we worked up a sweat on that dance floor, and he eventually did touch me, swinging me around and even rocking with me, slowly, his hips brushing—just barely—against mine, it all came back to me in a rush.

I used to dance with Seth a lot. Mainly because the other guys in the band didn't dance. Dylan had two left feet on a dance floor, Zane just wasn't that into dancing, and Jesse... well, Jesse pretty much preferred to watch.

So I would find myself dancing with Seth at parties and bars when we hung out, because I liked having a man to dance with. Someone who was really good at it, but who I didn't have to worry was gonna grope me. So I could just be free to lose myself in the music.

Though I never really thought to wonder, until now, why Seth would always dance with *me*.

I just assumed he loved to dance.

He'd touched me, sometimes, while we were dancing—to spin me around or dip me when we were goofing off, or lead me deeper into the crowd, or whatever. But that was it. He'd never even *tried* to grope me back then.

Just like he didn't tonight.

But back then, it didn't bother me that Seth didn't try to grope me. The possibility of being groped by Seth just wasn't on my radar. Maybe it was just me being a slightly naive nineteen-year-old, but I really didn't think it had occurred to him to be interested in me that way.

Or maybe it just hadn't occurred to me that he might be.

Back then, it hadn't occurred to me to try to grope him, either.

Why not?

I had that question stuck in my mind as I danced with Seth now. As I watched his hooded, smoky eyes... the way they moved over me. The way he watched me dance, like he was kinda trying not to. Like he couldn't resist watching.

Then I remembered.

Because he was a junkie.

And even if he wasn't... I had that pesky little rule about not getting involved with my bandmates. A rule that, admittedly, Zane had butted up against more than once when we were teenagers and didn't yet know each other well. When he'd tried to hit that—and failed. But Zane had never been as respectful about such things as Seth.

And then, of course, there was Jesse.

I'd had a crush on Jesse Mayes since pretty much day one. But the same rule I applied to Zane, and Seth, and Dylan, had to apply to Jesse. Until it didn't... and two years ago, I jumped off that cliff with him.

Bottoming out on that, alone—after Jesse dumped me—hardly felt worth it now.

Would it be worth it in the morning if I jumped Seth Brothers tonight?

My cocktail-buzzed mind had no answer to that.

So we danced and we danced... and then, eventually, we went back to the house and I went to bed.

Alone.

CHAPTER FOURTEEN

Seth

I HAD no idea what to make of it.

I flopped, naked, on my bed in the guest cottage. The lights were off, but there were lanterns hanging on the little patio outside, casting a glow. Everyone else had gone to bed a while ago, but I'd sat up, out there in the dark, just thinking. Unable to sleep.

Unable to decode the messages Elle was sending.

Officially, my discord with Dirty was no longer the main cause of my unease.

It was Elle.

Maybe I'd never really been able to read her. Maybe I'd never been all that great at understanding women at all... but I knew when a woman wanted me.

Elle, I could not understand.

Why she was being so cool to me.

Why she'd danced with me tonight, like... like she was attracted to me.

But maybe it was just dancing?

Maybe she was just having fun, and got a little carried away when her hands slid south of my hips and landed on my ass.

Maybe she didn't realize her pussy kept rubbing up against my thigh as she semi-dry-humped me, that I could feel her warm softness through the thin fabric of my pants.

Maybe she didn't feel my raging hard-on when she pressed herself up against me during that last slow song.

I had no fucking idea. For all I knew, maybe she was just drunk.

Maybe she really was lonely and none of what happened tonight was even about me.

Maybe that was how she danced with every guy these days, and it meant nothing at all.

Worse... maybe she saw me like she'd always seen Dylan—as a platonic male friend, one she could trust *not* to feel her up the first chance he got.

Or maybe she was just trying really, really hard to make amends for the past and rebuild the friendship we'd once had. If that was the case, I was not gonna piss all over her efforts like a fucking idiot by making a move on her.

I'd be lucky to count Elle as a friend.

The last thing I needed was for her to decide she'd made a giant mistake bringing me here because I'd started thinking with my dick. Because there was no way that was what she wanted. I was pretty fucking sure about that.

Though I really wasn't sure about much else.

Sometimes when she looked at me... I couldn't have guessed what she was thinking to save my life.

I did not remember her like this. So... guarded. So measured in everything she did. Carefully choosing her words and her facial expressions. The way she held herself, like a woman who was far too accustomed to having the world watch—and judge—her every move.

When she was younger, she was much more carefree. Like she was tonight.

But then again, maybe I just didn't remember things right.

I could not remember ever being confused about Elle's intentions back then—about what she thought of me or how she felt about me.

I could not remember ever thinking I might have any sort of chance with her.

From the beginning, it had been clear to me I had no chance whatsoever with Elle. Elle Delacroix was off-limits. Zane had told me as much the very day I met him, before he introduced me to the band. That was one of the ground rules.

Number one: Jesse is lead guitar.

Number two: You don't disrespect Dolly. That was Zane's grandma, who let the band practice in her garage.

And number three: No one fucks around with Elle.

I didn't have any problem with those rules, even after I met Elle. It wasn't as if I was the only one who noticed how pretty she was; everyone seemed to be crushing on her back then. Everyone, oddly, but Jesse. So it hardly seemed to matter. She had a boyfriend when I met her anyway. And she wasn't interested in me; not that I ever knew of.

So she was off-limits for several reasons.

Over the years, that list of reasons had only grown longer.

But tonight... dancing with her at that bar... the limits had seemed to evaporate.

Why?

Because she wanted me seemed like far too much of a stretch of the imagination.

Wishful fucking thinking.

And yet... I had been wishing it. Thinking about it...

Elle, slithering up against me, her hands roaming over my body as we danced... sliding downward... and the crowd dissolving around us, so we were alone. Alone and our bodies pressed together, for the first time, ever.

And my hands, moving over her body... drifting up her slender curves... her bare neck... over her face. Touching her mouth...

Jesus.

She was so fucking gorgeous. It wasn't exactly making this easier. Things were already hard enough. I wanted back in the band so bad I could taste it. So bad, it kept me up at night.

And now I wanted Elle.

Just as badly.

No. Actually... there were moments, like when she took hold of my hands at the photo shoot this morning... when she wrapped herself around me tonight and I felt her heat, and I smelled her warm, coconuty smell... when she pressed in close to talk to me over the music and I could almost taste her soft lips... I probably would've told every other member of Dirty to go fuck themselves if that's what it took to get her naked.

I knew there wasn't much blood left in my head right now, so my capacity for making solid decisions was kinda out the window, but if I could take Elle to bed... If she wanted me, right now, in her bed... I'd probably give it all up. Any chance of ever getting Dirty back.

Because if I slept with Elle, I did not see that happening.

Bad enough she'd already had a relationship with Jesse, and a breakup. Bad enough they all fucking hated me. Me, having sex with Elle, was hardly gonna lessen the drama with the band.

And still... it was all I could think about.

Elle. Naked.

After seeing her in that bikini, I could too easily picture her that way. Her smooth, tanned skin. Her slender, toned legs.

Her rosy nipples, in my mouth...

Fuck...

What would she sound like if I fucked her? If I was inside her...?

Would she gasp? Would she pant? Would she scream?

Would she shove me on my back and take the lead?

Would she want me to lead?

Would she want it hard? Or slow and easy...?

I had no idea... but I was imagining it all now. Curious... I was so fucking curious about her. My cock was aching with curiosity.

I grabbed it now; I was rock-hard. Sprawled on top of the sheets, the warm ocean air from the open window breezed over me. Elle was up there, in the house, and I started jerking myself off, thinking about her in her bed.

Just like I used to.

I stroked my hand along my hard length, up and down, slowly, and rolled my palm over the head.

Then I groaned and slowed my hand.

What the hell was I doing?

I stopped and took a breath. I tucked my hands behind my head and tried to think about something else as my cock pulsed. I closed my eyes and listened to the distant, almost musical rhythm of the waves. The chirp and twitch of insects in the trees.

It was wrong, jerking off here. I was a guest. Just seemed like an asshole thing to do.

But the damage had already been done...

All the blood in my brain had fled south, and my dick was throbbing almost painfully. My balls ached. No matter how I tried to change the direction of my thoughts, my cock won the argument.

So maybe I was an asshole.

I got up and went outside. Closed myself into the outdoor shower in the dark. I got the water running warm and stood under it, tried to catch my breath and calm down. I was so wound up, I was practically panting.

Shit. I so wanted her...

My hand was on my dick again, and it was all over. I had to come.

Badly.

It was probably better that I do this anyway, so I could think straight when I saw Elle tomorrow.

Maybe...

Because as the hours passed, I'd become increasingly unable to think of much at all besides her tanned skin, her gray eyes, her hesitant smile. And her tight, heart-shaped ass. Her firm tits. Her nipples... The rosy-pink color of them, glimpsed through the holes in her bikini.

And the glimpse of that bare pink pussy between her legs...

I came, hard, clutching the overhead faucet so I wouldn't slip and fall on the wet stone floor; the explosion, white-hot, tore through me, and I clenched my teeth to stifle the groan.

In my head I was coming on *her*, in that bikini, and she was loving it... grabbing my cock to lick it off, lapping up my come...

Fuck. Me.

I wanted Elle.

I shuddered and collapsed against the shower wall.

I wanted her on her knees, sucking me off.

I wanted her bent over, ass in the air, taking my cock up that bare pink pussy.

I wanted her screaming on her back, begging me for more.

And as I came down from the intensity of that orgasm, the blood slowly returning to my brain... I wanted her to kiss me.

I knew it was self-destructive. The last thing I should want, if I had any hope of getting back the one thing I'd *always* wanted.

But I didn't care...

I wanted her soft, swollen lips to brush against mine, and her tongue to fill my mouth.

I wanted to taste her.

I wanted those steel-gray eyes looking up at me, and I wanted her smiling.

I wanted her whispering my name against my skin.

Seth...

I wanted her... and I wanted her to want me.

CHAPTER FIFTEEN

Elle

IN THE MIDDLE of the night, Summer called. Actually, it was almost morning where she was, in Vancouver, but Summer was a nocturnal creature. I could hear music and voices—a lot of them—in the background.

Lucky for her, I was wide awake. I hadn't been able to sleep. I'd just been lying here on the bed, my head throbbing with the memory of Hawaiian music and Seth's body grinding up against mine.

"You okay?" was the first thing she said to me.

Though I doubted she could hear me when I answered, "Where the hell are you?"

The noise dimmed as she shut herself into some room where she could hear me. "You broke up with Ash?"

I sighed, but I doubted she heard that, either. "We were never really together, Summer. You're having a party?"

"I know you weren't. But judging by the trail of empties he's leaving on my carpet, he obviously thought so. I just wanted to make sure you're okay. And yeah, I'm having a party. You know. It's a Sunday."

That was typical. *It's a Wednesday. It's a Monday. It's my quarter-birthday.* Summer never needed an actual reason to celebrate.

"So are you okay or what?" she pressed. "Don't think I didn't notice you never answered me on that."

"No," I told her. "I'm not okay. And everyone asking me if I'm okay just makes me feel less okay."

"I know. I know you hate everyone worrying about you. But shit, bitch... What's going on with Seth?"

"Nothing."

"Are you fucking him?" Leave it to Summer to cut right to the chase. "That's what everyone wants to know. I just have the balls to ask."

"I'm not talking to everyone," I said. "I'm talking to you."

"I know that, babe. It's a figure of speech. Have you seen his dick yet?"

"Is that another figure of speech?" I asked dryly.

"No. It's a question."

"I'm not fucking him."

"Maybe you should be. Everyone's gonna think it anyway. It's all over the worldwide web. You might as well have some fucking fun."

"If his dick's in the guest cottage and my pussy's over here," I said, "I don't see that happening."

"Please. He's not gonna kick you out of bed, Elle."

"How would you know?"

"Because I saw those pictures of the two of you, on the beach."

"Oh."

"Yeah." She laughed. "Plus, you know. You're super hot?"

"Why are you so keen to get me laid?"

"Because I'm always keen to get you laid."

That much was true. It had almost killed her that it took me nearly a year after Jesse to screw anyone.

"Look," she said. "If you're done with Ash, just please don't take a fucking year to line up your next piece of ass. Better yet, find several. You should have an entire fucking cocksquad at your disposal. You're a rock star, for Christ's sake. Time to start acting like one."

Right; Summer had been on me to "slut it up like a rock star" as long as I'd known her.

"Sorry to disappoint you," I said, just like I had many, many times. "I'm just a one-cock-at-a-time girl."

"Then find one and make it your bitch. And by the way, I do *not* wanna hear about the time you could've screwed Seth Brothers in Hawaii but didn't and now you regret it, for like, the next year of my life."

"You won't."

"Babe. It's me. I know how you obsess about these things."

"I do not."

"*Babe.*"

Fuck. She knew me too well.

I'd totally been lying here obsessing when she called.

"I didn't obsess about Ash," I said in my defense.

"That's true. Which was how I knew you weren't gonna keep him around for long."

"You did?"

"Of course I did."

"Ugh. I'm sorry…"

I rolled over, and the room rocked woozily around me. I groaned. I'd definitely had too many of those fruity cocktails; I was gonna feel it in the morning. I fucking hated hangovers. Couldn't even remember the last time I'd had one.

Yes, actually… I could. It was the morning after Jesse broke up with me. Worst hangover ever. Nothing to make you feel like someone had just flushed your heart down the toilet like having your head in one for an entire day.

"We should really be having this conversation in person," I told her. "I know you care about Ash…"

"And so do you. That doesn't mean either of us should feel guilty because we're not in love with him."

I sighed again. Relieved that she understood me so well, and that she wasn't upset about any of this. "I think I'm in love with you right now."

"Get on a plane," she said. "I'll show you a good time."

I laughed, but it came out as a hiccup. "I'm gonna get some sleep, okay? Or try to. I haven't been sleeping much. This shit with Ash, and with the band..."

"You sure about that? First member of your cocksquad could be waiting for you..."

"I'm pretty sure he's sleeping. It's like three in the morning."

"Even better. You can slip in and out like a wet dream. He won't even know you're there."

"That's... disturbing."

"Is Flynn there? What about Flynn?"

"I'm hanging up."

"Fine. But I'm having a party when you get back. I'll fill it with eligible hot dudes for you."

She would, too. Summer was kinda queen of the hot dudes party scene. Went hand-in-hand with being a shit-hot DJ; the girl had never wanted for a cocksquad of her own.

"Goodnight, party girl."

After we'd hung up, my phone jingled with a text message. It was from Summer; a black-and-white photo of Seth she'd obviously snagged from the internet. It was from his later days with Dirty; he was looking all angsty and cool, walking into a bar as people pawed at him. And there I was, in the background, climbing out of a limo.

Then she texted an emoji: a smiling cat face with hearts for eyes —our personal shorthand for *wet pussy*.

I groaned again and stashed the phone away.

🎸

I still couldn't sleep. The ceiling fan looped lazily overhead and I just stared at it, unable to shut off my brain.

I was obsessing, yes.

Not about what Summer had said, exactly. She'd been known to encourage me to have sex with pretty much every semi-attractive male who happened across my path since the day I met her, over five years ago now. Including the ones I was never, ever going to have sex with, such as Zane, Dylan, Brody and Jude, men who were far more family to me than potential fuckmates—no matter how attractive they were.

It was about the fact that, for once, I actually *wanted* the man in question.

Badly.

And that was a bad idea. Kinda like Ash had been a bad idea… though for different reasons.

This, in fact, was a worse idea.

Far, far worse.

So why wasn't that stopping me?

Why was I climbing out of bed, pulling on a T-shirt and panties and creeping down the stairs, as quietly as I could, like some high school girl sneaking out to bone her hot college boyfriend? There wasn't even anyone in the house.

I did not yet know what I was doing, other than walking the line… or wobbling over it, half-drunk and horny. I was going to stand in the living room and gaze out the window at the cottage where Seth slept like some fucking lame-ass stalker, and then I was gonna decide what to do.

And that's what I did.

I stood there in the dark, looking out at the lanterns dangling on his patio, aglow in the night. I pictured myself turning around, going right back upstairs, getting into bed and going to sleep. Waking up tomorrow with not one thing changed.

Instead, I drifted outside. Right through the non-existent wall, where the living room flowed out onto the patio, and down the little stone path that connected the big house to the guest cottages. Hoping and praying the entire way that I didn't run into Flynn on his nocturnal rounds. He'd probably think I was some paparazzo intruder and brain me with the barrel of his gun.

I stood in the glow of the lanterns on Seth's patio and looked around. The doors to Flynn's cottage and Joanie's were closed, but they were only screen doors. There was no sound but the wind in the trees, the faint roar of the ocean. At least I was lit up here, my platinum hair a dead giveaway in the lantern light; no way Flynn would accidentally shoot me. Though I would have to explain what I was doing here, stalking Seth.

No; fuck that. I didn't have to explain shit to Flynn. He worked for me, right?

So why was I so fucking nervous about getting caught?

Because this is wrong.

Because you shouldn't be doing this.

Because fucking around with Seth would be selfish and stupid.

While I was telling myself all of this, I tried his door. It was a sliding screen with a billowy curtain fluttering on the inside. It was unlocked, but I didn't slide it open.

Instead, I hesitated.

I pictured what would happen if I went inside.

Seth was of course sleeping; it was the middle of the night. He was lying on his bed, maybe naked, maybe draped in a sheet. As I approached, he woke up. He saw me. Maybe he said my name, with a question mark at the end of it. He watched as I slipped off my shirt. Then I slid into bed with him in my panties.

And no, he did not kick me out.

I took a breath. My heart was *racing*.

Christ, was there something wrong with me?

I turned and hightailed it back to the house, ran straight up the stairs, closed myself in my bedroom, and flopped into bed.

I'd promised myself, after Jesse, I wasn't going to do this.

I'd sworn to myself, up and down: *No more rock stars.*

Before Jesse, I'd had several other boyfriends—men who were in no way involved with the music industry. Smart, classy, stable men. Men who had money and a life of their own, but who treated me well. Like gold, actually.

There was Ritchie, the restaurateur.

There was Martin, the tech consultant.

There was John, the investor and philanthropist, who'd proposed to me. I'd turned him down.

And then... there was Jesse Mayes. The bad boy rock star who, for some reason, had become a fantasy that I could not shake. Somewhere toward the end of my relationship with John, the idea of Jesse and I getting together had taken hold, and I could not let it go until I made him mine.

And make him mine I did.

I went after him with the force of a small hurricane.

Then, predictably—or at least, it was predictable to everyone but me—Jesse broke my heart, as bad boys do.

After that, I spent a year in dating limbo, afraid to open myself up to anyone, to even let anyone get near enough to ask me on a date, much less touch me... And then, at Jesse's wedding, I ended up fucking the baddest bad boy rock star I knew. The man who arguably surpassed Zane for male slut of the year—which was saying a whole fucking hell of a lot.

Ashley Player was so not the man for me, and yet I'd fucked my way right over the line with him.

And now, I was actually thinking about doing it again... with Seth.

No. Not true. I wasn't thinking about doing it.

I was *aching* to do it.

I'd already broken my promise to myself with Ash, yes. Not only had I sworn myself off of rock stars, I'd very specifically sworn myself off of anyone like Jesse Mayes. Gorgeous. Famous. Tall, dark and egotistical. That was the recipe for heartbreak. Guitarists, specifically, were to be avoided at all costs. More specifically, if he played guitar and sang—double threat—I was to turn my ass around and run for the fucking hills.

Ash fit every one of those criteria, but Ash was just for sexy fun times. That's how I justified it, to make it somehow okay that I'd broken my promise to myself.

And now... Seth.

Seth fit every one of those criteria, too.

But I never saw it coming.

He was gorgeous, yes. Beautiful; I'd go so far as to say Seth was a beautiful man. Sexy, definitely. Famous, too, in his own way. He was tall, and now, with his sun-lightened locks cut off, he was even darkish. Except Seth didn't have the inflated ego of my last two lovers. He definitely had an ego when it came to his talent; a justifiable one. He had confidence and charisma. He had a certainty about himself, a solidness. There was something incredibly attractive about that ego, and not in the way that Jesse's was.

Jesse was flashy and devastating. A woman could feel it across a room—Jesse Mayes was a heartbreaker.

And Ash… Ash was exactly what his name told you he was. Ashley Player was a player.

Seth… I really couldn't say.

Seth was still a mystery.

Yet I could not even pretend to myself that somewhere along the way screwing super-hot rock stars hadn't become a hot spot for me. Like some nasty addiction I couldn't shake or deny; I knew it was bad for me. Dangerous. That it would only do me harm.

And yet… it was like I suddenly understood what all the fangirls were always losing their shit about.

Maybe because I'd never had sex before like it was with Jesse. So motherfucking *hot*. I was just so fucking into him. Shitty for me, he didn't exactly feel the same way. And the flip side of being totally fucking infatuated with him was the devastation I felt when he rejected me—a pain like nothing I'd ever known.

I'd never had my heart broken before. Not even close.

And still, here I was, wanting it again; that high of wanting someone that badly.

If only I could have it without the crushing low of the breakup at the end.

I wondered… Was this anything close to what Seth experienced when he felt the urge to get high, even though he knew what the aftermath, the flip side of it, would be?

Even as the heartbreak of the breakup had sent me screaming

down a rollercoaster of emotional chaos, I'd managed to resist the urge: there were days I wanted to somehow get Jesse into bed with me, one last time, so I could fuck all my anger and hurt out—as if that would help anything. There were days when all I wanted to do was grab the nearest hot rock star, no matter who he was, and fuck him instead. There were days when I believed no one worthwhile would ever want me again. That I would never feel about anyone the way I felt about him.

I felt used, damaged and broken. Discarded.

And then there was Ash.

With Ash, the sex was scorching hot, but it was empty. A quick fix, meaningless. I didn't want to own his heart like I'd wanted Jesse's.

And in that, there was a different kind of suffering. I was realizing that now.

There were days, after I'd slept with Ash, that I felt like shit. Like I was only hurting myself.

And yet... I kept doing it.

And now here I was... and I had no idea what it would be like if I crossed that line with Seth. How far I might fall for him, or wouldn't. How badly he might hurt me, or I might hurt him.

The only thing I knew for sure: if Seth and I had sex, we were both getting hurt.

Him, because it would only complicate things between him and the rest of the band.

Me, because my heart hadn't fully healed. I was over Jesse, but I still wasn't whole. I'd gotten *past* the heartbreak, but I hadn't yet figured out how to put myself back together in the wake of getting smashed apart.

The fact was, I had no experience with how to do this, and apparently there was a fucking steep learning curve.

I still did not know when or how I would come out on the other side of this, feeling whole and stable and just fucking normal again.

I'd finally let go of the past, yet when I thought about getting emotionally involved with anyone again, I still felt broken.

I was unsure of my readiness to fall in love again.

And, simply put, I could not predict how my heart would react to having Seth Brothers, naked, in my bed.

If we had sex and—best case scenario—the sex was amazing... even if I felt wonderful right afterward... I did not know what would happen next.

I might turn into an ice queen. Freeze up. Become cold and distant.

I'd done that to men before.

I could also fall head-over-heels.

I'd done that before, too.

I seriously had no idea. And it was scary how out of control this made me feel.

Scarier still that it wasn't immediately turning me off of the idea. That it wasn't making me run for the hills.

That for some reason, it was just making me want to dive down that rabbit hole even more, and see where it went.

CHAPTER SIXTEEN

Elle

"YOU SURE YOU don't wanna see these?" Joanie asked me. She was on her laptop, on the other side of the island in Woo's kitchen, the screen turned away from me. "Are you absolutely sure? I'm telling you... you look *good*."

"I'll take your word for it."

I was hungover, nursing a glass of water and preparing to take my lunch outside. I'd only gotten up half an hour ago. I knew the photos of Seth and I from yesterday were all over the web by now. But I didn't particularly want to see them.

If I saw them, it would just beg the question of what everyone else was thinking when they saw them... and I didn't want to care about that.

"Seth looks good," Joanie added, glancing at me.

I narrowed my eyes at her; I did not appreciate her getting *that* familiar with me. Joanie had worked for me for several years now. I'd say we were friends. She knew almost every personal detail about my life, and I trusted her with those details. But that didn't mean I wanted her sticking her nose into my relationships with men.

She gave me a cheeky look right back and went back to her computer.

I sighed. "Fine. Turn it here."

She dutifully spun her laptop around. On the screen was a webpage open to a photo of me and Seth at the beach. And he did look good.

He also looked like he was my man.

We were holding hands, just barely, our fingers touching... and we weren't even looking at each other. But there was something there, in that touch. In our body language. Something gut-deep, almost tangible.

I didn't realize it when it happened. That what I'd been feeling, standing there with Seth, would come pouring through the photo the way it did...

Chemistry.

Connection.

And I had this kind of saucy, *Fuck the world* look on my face. Because that's exactly what I'd been thinking when the photographer took that photo.

Fuck the world if they want to judge me for this.

I reached out, before I even knew what I was doing, and slammed the laptop shut. Joanie's eyes met mine. "Do you think there's any chance in hell that the internet will... I don't know... go up in smoke or something, before everyone sees that?"

"I think it's too late for that," she said.

As if on cue, her phone, sitting on the island between us, started to vibrate. It had been doing that a lot. Unable to resist, Joanie swiped it up and hightailed it out of the kitchen to answer the call where I couldn't hear her.

I took my lunch out on the back patio, alone. I had my phone with me but the ringer and vibrate mode were turned off. The calls had been coming in all morning; Joanie had told me so.

I still hadn't answered one of them.

And I realized, as I ate: I only actually cared about what one person thought of those photos. But I hadn't seen Seth yet.

When I asked Flynn if he'd seen him, he said Seth had gone down to the beach early and he hadn't come back. I did not know what that meant, if it meant anything.

When I finished eating, I gathered my courage and checked my texts. There were many, but I only opened one.

Ash: What the fuck is going on?

Okay; he was mad.

Maybe he had a right to be?

Maybe I'd somehow let him believe he had that right. Which meant I really had to set things straight. I decided to call him, and I really fucking hoped he'd pick up; I just had to get this over with.

"Elle," he said when he answered.

"Hi."

"You okay?"

"Yes." Why did everyone keep asking me that? Like Seth had abducted me and dragged me off to paradise? "You?"

"Not really. Just saw pictures of you holding hands with Seth at the fucking beach, so no, I'm not okay."

"Why?" I asked him.

"Because. You fucking know why. Are you fucking him now?"

I took a deep, slow breath. "Ash, it's none of your business."

"Since when?"

"Since when do you think it is your business?"

"I don't know, Elle. Maybe since you started fucking me?"

"As *friends*. You said it yourself. 'Friends with benefits.' You made me agree we weren't gonna mess with our friendship by fucking."

"So? That doesn't mean seven months later, when I'm the only guy you have been fucking, it's okay for you to run off with someone else without even fucking telling me."

"I didn't *run off*. And I don't have to tell you anything, Ash."

"So that's it? You're just blowing me off?"

"I'm not blowing you off. We're friends. That's all we've ever been."

"That's fucking bullshit, Elle."

"No. It's the truth." And finally, I said it. "There's nothing between us, Ash. Just... let it go."

There was an awful, crushing silence on the other end of the line.

Then he hung up.

That was when I felt it; someone standing close behind me.

I turned to find Seth holding two mugs of coffee. He reached to set one down on the table in front of me.

"Thanks," I managed, setting my phone aside.

Seth stood there looking uncertain, maybe wondering if I wanted to be alone. But right now, the last thing I wanted was to be alone. If I was alone, all I'd hear in my head was that conversation. And that horrible silence.

The sound of Ash hanging up on me.

"You can sit down, if you want."

Seth sat in the chair opposite me. He didn't seem to want to look me in the eyes though, his gaze stuck on his mug.

How much of that conversation had he heard?

"I'm gonna head up to Vancouver," he said to his coffee. "You know... I owe Ray that visit."

I didn't know what to say; that was kinda the last thing I expected him to say. "Oh. Okay?"

"I booked a flight out." Finally, he looked up at me. "Today."

"You booked a flight?" I repeated, stunned. "When?"

"Last night."

"Last night...? Before we went dancing?"

His eyes slowly darkened, maybe recalling the way we'd steamed up that dance floor. He shook his head a little. "In the middle of the night."

"In the middle of the night?" *Damn.* That came out... bitchy. Weirdly high-pitched.

I was starting to freak out. My lunch sat in a glob in my stomach.

"I'm heading to the airport in a few minutes. You know... I should get back..." He trailed off.

"Oh," I said, again. "Okay..." I had no idea what he needed to get back to, but suddenly I felt weirdly betrayed. Like there were all these things about his life I didn't know, but maybe I should know... and yet, I had no real right to know.

I was getting pissed off, actually. Anger; a knee-jerk reaction to him leaving and me not knowing what the fuck to do about it.

I couldn't do anything about it. He didn't owe me anything.

But I didn't want him to go. Not yet.

"Do you have to go?" I asked, desperate for some excuse to slow his departure. "I mean, I'm staying a few more days. We could fly back together." I'd been planning to stay as long as I could; maybe longer than I'd originally intended. I'd spoken to Woo yesterday, and he'd assured me I could stay forever. "Woo doesn't mind," I told him, though I knew the real reason I'd become so comfortable here, and it had little to do with Woo's open door hospitality.

It was all Seth.

"That's not a good idea, Elle," he said, his voice a little rough, but his gaze steady on mine.

"Why? Is this... Is this about the pictures?"

"It's not about the pictures."

"Did someone say something to you?" Shit, did someone call him and threaten him or something? One of the guys in the band? Brody? Ash?

"Elle... I don't want to cause you any more trouble than I already have."

"You're not causing trouble, Seth," I insisted. "It's trouble that was always there."

"I'm not making it any better."

"Actually," I found myself saying, "you are. It's been great having you here."

"I'm sure Ash would see it differently."

"I don't care how Ash sees it."

Our eyes were still locked. I couldn't quite read the look on his face, other than the fact that something was telling me he did not actually want to go. He was just trying to do the right thing.

And something deep inside me twisted inside-out.

"I want to thank you, for what you've done for me," he said, in a soft, low voice. "Bringing me here. Talking to me. Extending that olive branch."

"You don't have to thank me, Seth."

Silence.

And yes, there was something in his eyes. Something he wasn't saying. Something that was absolutely burning with need.

It wasn't the same need I'd seen in his eyes before, back at the audition: the need for redemption, acceptance.

This was something else.

And I felt it, too.

"Thank you," he repeated.

Then he looked away. He stood, and I watched him turn and head into the house. He hadn't even drank his coffee.

And that was it.

Seth was gone.

🎸

Mid-afternoon, the intensity of the sun drove me off the beach; it was crazy-hot today. I made my way back up the rocky path through the trees in my bare feet, slowly, enjoying the fragrant, coolish air between the trees. Or trying to enjoy it.

I was wearing a light, lacy cover-up over my bikini, and it was fluttering around me in the breeze. This feeling; this was why I came to Hawaii. Peace. Quiet. And that ever-present ease in the air, the smell of the ocean, the flawless blue skies.

Paradise.

And yet, with Seth gone... it didn't feel the way it should anymore. I just couldn't absorb any of it.

I'd spent an hour on the beach, alone, and I couldn't relax. I couldn't stop wondering if there was something I should've done differently, said differently, to somehow make him stay.

It was a dangerous line of thought. Too close to the questions I'd asked myself in the days and weeks, and even months, after Jesse left me.

I'd been avoiding my phone since that phone call with Ash, but now, as I reached the top of the path and stepped through the trees, I realized maybe I should've been answering it.

Because there was a camera crew in Woo's yard.

It was Liv, standing on the back patio with Joanie, and a camera guy sitting nearby, tinkering with his camera, setting it up on a tripod.

"Fuck." I stopped up short. "Seriously?"

Flynn, who'd been trailing silently in my wake, stepped past me. "I'll get rid of them."

"No." I caught his arm, stopping him. "I want to see what she wants."

I already knew what Liv wanted. More "sound bites" for the documentary series. And if she'd come all the way here, to talk to me, when there were plenty of other band members closer to where she was that she could be harassing... this was about Seth.

As I stepped through the gate, they all saw me and Liv smiled.

"They just got here," Joanie explained, hurrying over to me, probably expecting me to be pissed. I wrapped my cover-up around me as I approached, though they weren't filming. "I was just on my way down to tell you. You weren't answering your phone..."

"The tripod's a tad presumptuous, Liv," I told her as I reached her on the patio. I wasn't in the mood for small talk, and I didn't want her to think crashing my vacation time with a camera was in any way okay with me.

Brody would be hearing about this.

"Well," Liv said, "I was hoping I could get that footage. You know, you, on camera, sharing your thoughts about Seth Brothers and whatever's going on between him and Dirty."

"You should've called."

"I did," she said. "So did Brody."

Great. So Brody knew about this. Approved it, maybe. He'd definitely be hearing about this.

"I have nothing to say right now. I'm on vacation."

"I realize that," Liv said. "And I'm sorry. But the band is planning to resume auditions as soon as you're back, and the footage of Seth's audition is likely going in the show, which means I need someone to talk to me about it. And since you came here with him, I figured, you and he must be..." She trailed off. Apparently, even Liv didn't have the stones to outright accuse me of screwing Seth. "Friends?" she finished.

"I told you. I have nothing to say."

"Right. But obviously you have an opinion."

"An opinion I'm not prepared to share at this time." I could feel Flynn hovering, edging closer. Just itching to interject and escort Liv and her guys off the property.

A couple of other crew guys had appeared around the side of the house, hauling equipment bags. They held back, observing the negotiation.

But Liv was not backing down.

"This is an important part of the process, Elle. I understand that you're on vacation, but Brody and I discussed it, and we both felt you'd be the best person to comment on Seth's position with the band—"

"Seth doesn't have a position with the band," I said. All the while, my head was fucking reeling. *Brody and I?* What the fuck was Brody doing, sending her here to accost me?

"And if that's the case," she said, "all I need is for you to say so, on camera, and we'll be on our way."

I doubted that. As soon as she got me in front of that camera, she'd be digging for more. I couldn't really fault Liv; she was just trying to make a killer TV series. Doing her job.

But right now, I didn't care about that.

I really didn't need her showing up here, right when I was feeling so fucking vulnerable—having Seth here, having Seth leave...

and having no idea what to do about all these feelings he'd stirred up in me. The very last thing I needed was a camera crew in my face.

But I would play the game.

I wasn't going to have Flynn throw her out. I was going to make her turn around and leave. Voluntarily.

"Listen to me, Liv. This has nothing to do with Dirty or finding our new guitarist."

"Then let's talk about that."

"We are talking. But not on camera."

Liv considered that. Then she said, "Seth already talked to me. On camera."

What?

"When?"

"We caught him at the airport, when we landed. Total fluke."

I stared at Liv for a long, long moment. She didn't flinch.

I believed her, maybe, about the fluke of running into Seth. Either way, though, interviewing him was no fluke.

"Alright," I said, because she'd caught me off-guard. I didn't love it, but I definitely didn't like Seth talking to her, and me without a chance to respond.

I wasn't planning to ask Liv what he'd said. I didn't like what asking might imply—that I was worried about what he'd said about me.

So I simply said, "I'll give you the interview. When I'm ready."

🎸

Two hours later, I was ready enough. Joanie had called in a hair and makeup team from among the many contacts she kept on the island. I'd gotten dressed, had my hair and makeup done, and rejoined Liv and her crew on the patio. They'd set up in the shade, the ocean view in the background, and were ready for me.

I sat down and we started rolling. I knew it wasn't gonna be easy. I knew Liv was gonna dig. And dig she did... After some bullshit small talk about the audition process overall, she went straight for it.

"Tell me about Seth."

But this was far from my first rodeo. I wasn't gonna give up anything I didn't want to give.

"What do you want to know?" I asked her.

"What do you think of him?" Liv sat across from me, next to the camera, feeding me questions. It was her job to get content out of me; content she could use. I knew whatever she said wouldn't be included in the show, but anything I said might be.

"I think he's our ex-guitarist."

Liv sighed a little. "Come on, Elle. This is a documentary. I'm not grilling you for some junk entertainment gossip show. This is the real you, right?"

"It's the real me," I said.

"Then tell me what you really think of Seth Brothers."

"I think Seth Brothers is an extremely talented musician," I said.

"Okay. Now tell me about the man, not the musician."

"Are you gonna tell me what he said about me?" I asked, breaking form. Because for the last two hours it had been killing me. I wanted to ask her, without coming right out and actually asking her.

"You really want to know?" she said. And there was something about the way she said it that rubbed me entirely the wrong way.

Like there was something to know. Something I should know?

Something I wouldn't want to know?

Yeah. This was a mistake.

Since when had this documentary become an inquisition about my feelings toward Seth Brothers?

"This interview is over." I got up. I started to walk away, heading into the house, but turned back. The camera was still filming; the camera operator had swiveled it around to film my exit. "Turn the camera off." I directed this straight at the camera op. He glanced at Liv, and Liv nodded.

He stopped rolling.

"You know I'm gonna hear what you asked him anyway," I told

her, "when I watch the dailies. That's in my contract. I get all the dailies."

"Uh-huh. So does he."

"What?"

"Seth's negotiating a deal with the network."

"Since when?"

"Since this morning. When I interviewed him at the airport." Liv shrugged, like this was no big thing. To be expected, even. "The network wanted to talk to him before they'd let me interview him. Turns out they want his side of the story."

I just stared at her.

What the *fuck* was going on?

"You know," Liv said, "there are two sides to every rock 'n' roll story..."

I was already walking away.

"I mean, your story is the one everyone cares about, of course," she backpedaled, following me into the house. But while I jetted straight for the stairs, Flynn stepped in to stop Liv in her tracks. "Come on, Elle! You know what I mean!" she called after me, but I wasn't listening.

My phone was already dialing.

"Brody!" I said when he answered. "What the fuck. Seth's in the documentary now?" I wasn't even sure why it bothered me so much. My mind was spinning in every direction at once as I closed myself into the bedroom.

"Apparently," Brody said. "We've decided to roll with it."

"*We?*"

"We're gonna let the network do a contract with Seth," he continued, "and see how it plays out."

"He gets the dailies?"

"Who cares? The band gets approval on the final cut anyway."

I could not believe it. "Why didn't you tell me?"

And why didn't Seth tell me? He could've called me from the airport, or messaged me to at least give me a heads up about Liv.

Except... he didn't have my number.

How would he? I'd never given it to him.

"I did," Brody said. "Check your messages once in a while."

I ripped open the bedroom door, about to call out for Joanie—but she was standing right there, poised to knock, looking sheepish as fuck.

"Talk later." I hung up on Brody. "Brody called?"

"Yeah," Joanie said, her eyes wide. "He called this afternoon. Several times. Something about Seth and the documentary? He wants you to call him back. But you told me no calls... *especially* from Brody..." She trailed off. "Shit. What's wrong?"

"Nothing." She was right, I did tell her that. Repeatedly. "Just get me a flight home."

"To L.A.?"

"No," I said. "Vancouver."

I had no idea if the auditions Liv had mentioned were about to get underway in L.A. or Vancouver, since, clearly, I hadn't been checking my messages. I wasn't even sure where all the members of my band were right now.

All I knew for sure was that Seth was in Vancouver.

CHAPTER SEVENTEEN

Elle

WHEN THE PLANE LANDED, Flynn loaded us into a car and drove me to my place in Lions Bay, just north of the city. We passed Joanie's place in downtown Vancouver on the way and dropped her off.

As soon as Flynn dropped me at my house, alone, I opened my laptop and found the email from the post-production supervisor on the documentary series. She'd already sent out today's dailies.

I carried the laptop upstairs to my bedroom, kicking off my sandals. I curled up on my bed in the dark and clicked the link in the email. It took me to an FTP site, where I could download the video I wanted.

I hadn't even bothered to bring my other things upstairs; my bags sat in the foyer where Flynn put them. I didn't get changed or eat anything or even turn on a light.

Beyond the first day of filming on this series, I hadn't even bothered to watch the dailies.

But I watched Seth's interview footage now.

He was standing in the shade, his sunglasses pushed up on top of his head. A palm tree swayed in the background. Liv, off-camera, fed him questions, like she'd done with me, and she left no stone unturned.

She asked Seth about his addiction, about his difficult path to recovery, about his overdose, about both times he'd been fired from Dirty. She asked about the reunion show earlier this year and his audition last week.

Lucky for Liv, Seth was much more forthcoming in his interview than I'd been. And he answered every question the same way he'd answered me when I'd asked.

She also asked him about every member of Dirty.

About Jesse, he said, "Jesse is the best guitarist I've ever played with. Anyone can see why the fans love him. He's the total package."

About Dylan, he said, "Dylan's a madman on the drums and as solid as they come."

And about Zane, he said, "Tell me one thing you dislike about Zane Traynor and I'll tell you five things to love about him."

To which Liv said, "Some would say he's a womanizer."

And Seth replied, "Yeah. Well, he's also fucking brilliant. He's sharp as a fucking razor, passionate, totally committed, and no one will make you laugh harder when you're having a shitty day. And I'll tell you something else people don't give him credit for. He's got vision, and he goes after that vision like a tornado."

"That's seven things," Liv said.

"Seven true things. Zane's got a reputation, right? For being a cocky asshole. Maybe that reputation is deserved. But not many people really know Zane. There's a lot more there than meets the eye. If it weren't for Zane, Dirty wouldn't be the band they are today. They might never have gotten off the ground. They'd probably have ended up just another garage band that became just another bar band playing endless cover songs to fifty people a night."

Well.

Jesse was not gonna love that. Not sure I did either.

Yet I respected Seth for saying it. Whether it was strictly true or not, it was his opinion, clearly, and he was standing by it.

"What about Elle?" Liv asked.

"Elle is the best bassist I've ever played with, by miles," was his answer.

"How so?"

"Well, a lot of bass players end up picking up the bass by default. They start out as guitarists, but migrate to bass because the band needs a bassist. And they never really bring anything sensational to their instrument. They're just laying down that bass line, and if you're not even conscious of hearing them in the song, they've pretty much done their job. But then there's that rarer breed of musician who was just born to play the bass. Elle is one of those. She just feels it, you know? She brings the funk to Dirty in a big way. If not for her, they'd just be another group of white guys rocking out. And who needs that, right?"

Liv actually laughed in the background. "Can I play that back for them?"

Seth smiled a little and shrugged. "Do what you've gotta do."

"Okay," she said. "Now tell us something we don't know about Elle."

Seth went silent. He looked off, maybe trying to think of something. Maybe choosing his words. I noticed, though, he didn't hesitate this long to sum up the other band members.

Finally, he said, "Elle's got this thing about her. It's like two sides of a coin. Hot and cold. Strength and vulnerability. It's always been there. Makes you want to protect her, and at the same time, set her loose, see what she can do. She probably has the most untapped potential of anyone in the band. She's the most diverse. That's why her solo album was such a success. Why she's able to dip her finger into so many pies and find success, again and again. No matter what happens with Dirty, you'll be seeing a lot of Elle in years to come. She's got staying power and the ability to grow and evolve."

"And what about that hot-cold thing?" Liv asked. "I've heard people say that about her before. Can you elaborate?"

"It's like I said, it's two sides of the same coin. Or maybe it's a double-edged sword. It's that thing that makes her hard to know. That thing that makes guys want her and girls want to be like her. She's fierce, and she's fragile. She's real. You sit her down in an interview and ask her a bunch of prefab questions, you're not gonna get the real Elle. But put her onstage and you'll see her pouring out everything she's got through the music, she's sweating, breaking down in tears, and that's just her. That's where you'll find her, at that intersection between the real person and the rock star. But how do you touch that? It scares some people, I think. She's kinda like Zane that way, I guess. The two of them are kinda larger than life. They're hyper-real. If you really want to know them, you gotta be fearless. I don't think many people are that fearless."

"And how about the other guys?" Liv asked. "Would you describe them like that? 'Larger than life'?"

"Not exactly. Jesse's a star. No doubt about that. But you can get to know him. As long as you can get him to sit still long enough. And Dylan you can get to know, if you can keep his attention long enough."

"And how about you?"

Seth shook his head, and in that moment, I could feel that the interview was over. It was the last question he was going to answer for Liv. "Me?" he said. "I'm just a regular guy, who likes to play guitar. That's all I've got, Liv. I've got a plane to catch."

The video ended.

I played it again, from start to finish. Then I played it again.

I listened, carefully, to everything Seth said about himself, about the band, and about me. And with every word he said, with every new thing I learned about Seth, I liked him more.

He intrigued me. And it worried me that he intrigued me so much.

But it did not freak me out as much as it should.

I wasn't sure what to think. What to do. I did not know what this was... This strange flow of feelings beginning to build in me. This growing thing.

It was more than mere sexual attraction, though.

A curiosity?

An infatuation?

I did not know what I was getting into. But the fact was, I'd followed him here. I'd flown to Vancouver for one reason only: because I knew Seth was here.

And yet, I didn't call him. I didn't reach out.

I did not yet know if I would.

Frankly, I was scared. I was scared of looking into the eyes of a man who seemed to understand me so well, and who had the courage to say so, in front of the world... no matter how it might come back to hurt him.

The next day, midway through the afternoon, my drummer showed up at my house. On a boat.

He pulled up to the dock at my neighbor's place, which I knew because she called me all in a fluster to tell me. After working his charms and getting her permission to moor there, he came on up to see me.

"Good timing," I told him as I let him in. "Just got back from a meeting with my publicist."

"Cool." Dylan swept me up into a hug with his long, strong drummer's arms. I nestled into the warmth of his T-shirt, his solid chest, and I felt... a little better. Like things were going to be okay.

Maybe.

Since we were teenagers and played in our first band together—just before Brody recruited the two of us to join Zane and Jesse's band, and we formed Dirty—Dylan had been one of my very best friends. I was closer to him than anyone else in the band. Even Jesse.

When he released me, he looked me over and I felt weirdly exposed, like he could see everything I'd been thinking these past few days. Like he could tell I'd been lusting after Seth Brothers.

He narrowed his eyes at me a little. "You don't look like someone who just got back from Hawaii."

"To be honest, I don't feel like one."

He trailed me through the house as we headed out to the back deck. The back of the house looked west, over the waters of Howe Sound, the blue-gray humps of Gambier and Bowen Island in the distance—which was the main reason I'd bought this place. I could never get tired of that view. Gazing out at the water had a settling, resetting affect on me, at once inspiring and therapeutic... much like music did.

Dylan had brought beers and stashed them in the fridge, bringing two bottles outside for us. He popped them open and handed one to me as we sank into a couple of my lounge chairs. He'd stripped off his shirt and kicked off his shoes along the way, and now wore nothing but his shorts. They were jean shorts; ragged, faded cut-offs that ended halfway down his muscular thighs, splattered with paint and streaked with sawdust.

I smirked. "What's with the never nudes?" It was a term we'd appropriated from the TV show *Arrested Development*, where one of the characters wore cut-offs at all times because he had a fear of being nude.

"Huh?" He followed my gaze to his cut-offs. "Oh. Been working on the cabin with Ash."

"Uh-huh." I happened to know that the "cabin" was a veritable mansion on one of the Gulf Islands, just off the coast. Dylan had bought it recently. "Renovating?"

"Converting half of the garage into a man-cave for Ash."

Well, that explained the paint and sawdust. "Je-sus," I joked, "are you two gonna get married, or what?"

"Maybe." He swigged his beer and looked at me. "You cut him loose, huh?"

I rolled my eyes. "He wasn't mine to cut, Dylan."

"Right."

"He still over there?"

"Yeah." Dylan looked out over the water in the general direction of his "cabin," though the island couldn't be seen from here. It was close, but too far south. "He's drowning his sorrows in hard labor."

God. I did not want to think about Ash's sorrows. But at the same time, I cared. I didn't want him experiencing any sorrow whatsoever over me.

I knew I'd have to talk to him about it. Soon. I'd been the one who insisted we were only friends. Which meant a friend was what I'd have to be. Though part of me thought he was being a little ridiculous, making more out of this than there ever was.

I didn't say all that to Dylan. Dylan had a special relationship with Ash, like a brother bond that went even deeper than what he had with Jesse and Zane. He'd be protective of Ash, and I had no idea what Ash had told him about "us."

I really didn't want to get into it with him, either.

I just watched him for a minute, stretched out on my lounge chair. His ruddy, slightly tanned skin. For a redhead, he tanned decently. His hair was dark auburn, but glinted all kinds of copper and red and gold in the sun. It flopped over his forehead in waves and curled around his ears. He had a straight nose and high, fashion-model cheekbones, a slight divot in his chin, and an underwear model's body—literally.

When we'd met, Dylan Cope had been a cute but gawky teenager, all flailing limbs, wailing on his drum kit. Somewhere over the years he'd grown into a total stud of a man. Women melted into puddles of giggling gush in his wake. And even I didn't mind occasionally checking him out.

I'd tried hooking him up with pretty much every available female I knew over the years. Sometimes with success, sometimes not. But even though Dylan was a total babe, I'd never felt even a twinge of *What if...?* the way I had with Jesse. I'd never once thought about hooking him up with *me*.

It was a personality thing. Dylan and I were nowhere near couple material, and we both knew it. Maybe it was my hot and cold personality. As a bandmate, he'd never been bothered by it. It just kinda rolled off his easygoing nature.

But as a couple? Disaster.

The truth was, Dylan was just *too* laid-back for me.

Usually.

He could, however, be coy, calculating, and far too aware of his own charms. Like right now. I knew he wanted the goods on Seth and Hawaii. But he wasn't outright asking.

As we had beers over the water, he just kept saying things like, *How was Woo's place?* and *You look like you got some sun...* and *Met anyone lately?*

"Are you ever just gonna come out and ask?" I asked him after my second beer.

"Ask what?"

"Dylan. Don't be an idiot."

"What?"

"Just ask me about Seth or whatever, so we can get past it."

"Okay," he said. "Tell me about Seth."

"Tell you what?"

"Why'd you take him to Hawaii?"

"To talk to him. We already went over this."

"What did you talk about?"

"Everything."

"You guys are cool now?"

"I'm not sure we were ever uncool... but yes. We're cool."

He nodded. "Cool. You know you shouldn't have done that, though."

"Done what?"

"Take him with you."

"Why the hell not?"

He sighed, looking exasperated. "Because it's just causing more shit with the band, Elle."

"I didn't cause shit," I said. "I did what I did. If the guys have their panties in a knot about it, that's their fucking problem."

His eyebrows rose, but he didn't say anything. It was enough to make me feel shitty.

Really shitty.

"Do not give me shit, Dylan. Do I ever give you shit about where you go, or with whom you go, or what you do on your time off?"

"Nope."

"Right. So shut it. You want another beer?"

"Yup."

And it pretty much went on like that for the rest of the day.

He brought it up, every once in a while, pointing out that we now had the fallout of this shit storm to deal with, but offering no suggestions on how to deal with it. Finally I asked him, "So what do you want me to do about it now? I can't turn back time."

And he said, "Maybe we should talk to Brody."

That was his answer for everything.

Let's talk to Brody.

Brody will have the answer.

Usually, he did. But on this one, I was hardly gonna defer to Brody.

"Let's just do the rest of the fucking auditions," I said, "and let the bullshit with Seth drop."

"Fine with me," he said. But after a minute he added, "Don't think Jesse's gonna let it drop, though."

"Jesse can bite me," I said, and Dylan finally shut up.

By now, I was pissed right off. I knew Dylan meant well. He was just concerned. Trying to do his part. Thinking that coming over to talk to me over beers before the next round of auditions would help.

It didn't.

It just made me feel more defensive of what I'd done, and more defensive of Seth. This was Dylan; he was gonna be the easiest on me, and it was already feeling hard. If he was having this much of a problem with what I'd done, what the hell was Jesse gonna say? Brody?

But I couldn't exactly start defending Seth to the guys without setting off warning bells—and another shit storm.

By the time Dylan left, I knew, by *how* defensive I felt of Seth, that I had to see him again. There was so much left undone there, and unsaid.

It took mere seconds from the time Dylan sped off in his boat for me to get Joanie on the phone.

"I'm gonna text you an address," I told her. "I need you to send a car there, to pick up Seth Brothers."

CHAPTER EIGHTEEN

Seth

I ARRIVED at Elle's place just as the sun was going down. It was a sprawling mansion on the coast, low white slabs and glass, hidden in the trees. By the time the car stopped in the driveway, I was wound right up. My heart was beating too hard. My palms were sweating.

All the way here, I'd been wondering what this was about—a car service showing up at Ray's place and the driver telling me he was supposed to take me to some house in Lions Bay, for Joanie.

I knew exactly whose house it would be.

As for why Elle had sent a car for me, there could only be one reason: she wasn't finished with me yet.

She didn't want me to leave Woo's place; she'd made that clear. She'd also said she was staying in Kauai for a few more days, but now here she was, the very next day. Either she was pissed at me, royally, or she wanted to see me for some other reason.

One look at her when she opened her front door told me what that reason was.

I stepped inside, feeling uneasy. I'd never been in this house before, but I barely looked around. There was a white entrance hall and a giant, sweeping staircase leading upstairs, behind her.